THE CHEMIST

Stephanie Colbert

creativewriting1956@

visit https://www.stephaniecolbert.co

Printed in the United States of America

Cover by Lotfy

ACKNOWLEDEMENTS

I would like to thank everyone in my life that has given me support and allowed me to pursue my passion.

Table of Contents

CHAPTER ONE

THE TRUTH WON'T SET YOU FREE

Katherine "Kat" Hope had just received a call from some nut-job who called himself "The Chemist." He claimed there was a woman's body located in an abandoned building in the Bronx. When she tried to get more information, he'd hung up. While she had other, more pressing stories on her desk, there was something in the man's voice that piqued her interest. Since she'd written that piece on Mark Garrett, she received crank calls every day. Even though she had almost finished another story, her gut instinct, told her to check it out—her gut was never wrong. She looked at the time; it was 10:30 a.m.

Kat glanced at Jimmy, her supervising editor. He was talking to another reporter inside his office. It was probably for the best that he was busy because he had become overprotective of her, ever since that day five years ago. But she couldn't afford to think about that now; she had a job to do. She left a message with Cindy, Jimmy's highly underpaid secretary, and simply said that she would be out investigating a lead. She didn't say where or why, because if Jimmy found out, he would have insisted she didn't go. And when she convinced him she was going anyway, he would have told her that she must have someone accompany her. More than likely that person would have proved to be a hindrance. But most importantly, she liked to work alone.

Kat tried to hail a cab but had to wait a few minutes. As she impatiently stood there, she paid no attention to the street vendor with his pastry cart, and the wonderful aromas emitting from it. Or the people coming and going across the street to Sam's Diner, where, due to its convenience, most people from the newspaper went. She paid no attention to the line of schoolchildren, their young faces filled with excitement as they waited to go on a tour of the newspaper. If she'd known that her life was about to change in unimaginable ways, she would have taken it all in and clung to it, for it would have brought solace when the horror became unbearable.

Finally, a cab stopped for her, and she hurriedly got in and gave the cab driver the address. She looked at his license. "Amir, I'm in a hurry so take whatever shortcuts you can."

"Lady, everyone is in a hurry these days," he said gruffly.

Like most people, Kat divided her day into two parts. Things she had to do, and the things she loved to do. But unlike most people, it was her job that fell into the latter category. She had been fascinated with writing as long as she could remember, but never dreamt that one day she would be working for the largest newspaper in New York City.

As usual, Kat didn't waste a minute. She reached inside her bag and took out her notebook and two pens, and then scanned her notes. After she finished, she made some phone calls, trying to look for something that could be her next big headline. There was still a lot of talk about her last one. Even veteran reporters were saying it was Pulitzer Prize winning material. Not one to rest on her laurels, she had become even more driven to produce the best, most accurately researched news in the city.

Most of her follow-up phone calls were a waste of time since they didn't interest her. Those leads she would give to Jimmy so that he could pass them on to other journalists. It was the series of articles that she did on Steve Perkins that earned her that privilege. He had stolen millions using a Pyramid Scheme, and a lot of people had suffered. But even as clever as he was, she was more so and had revealed the truth. Because of her exposé, the police finally had enough to make an arrest, and according to the District Attorney, his conviction was almost certain. But what she thought was more rewarding was the knowledge that a lot of people would at least have a portion of their hard-earned money returned to them.

Kat found two leads that sounded promising and made notes to herself about what would be the best angle to pursue to get the type of top quality story she was known for. “What am I doing on this wild goose chase when I have real stories to write about?” she said out loud without even realizing it.

“Did you say something?” asked the cab driver, Amir.

“What? No, just thinking out loud.”

Kat could see the strange look on his face when he gazed at her in his rear-view mirror. She ignored it. Immersed in her work, it took a while before she realized the taxi wasn’t moving. They couldn’t go anywhere because of the bumper-to-bumper traffic. “Isn’t there a faster route you can take?” she asked, even though she already knew the answer. Kat thought about the article waiting on her desk and wanted to get this over with so she could make it back in time.

Amir looked at her again; his face bore an expression of disdain.

“Lady, I’ve been driving these streets for over twenty-five years. If there were one, we’d be on it.”

“How much longer until we get there? As I told you, I’m pressed for time.”

“It’s about a fifteen-minute walk, but if you ain’t in the mood for a walk, in this traffic, it’ll take a while.” He seemed indifferent to her concerns.

As a New Yorker, she was used to the traffic. As a reporter, she found the situation to be untenable and decided to do something about it.

“How much do I owe you?”

He looked at his meter. “That’ll be $28.67.”

Kat gave him $35. "Keep the change."

"Thanks," he told her, seemingly unimpressed by her generosity.

Kat always wore sensible flats and today was just one of many days that she was glad she did. She grabbed her notebook and pens and put them in her oversize bag. In it was everything that, she had learned from experience, might come in handy. Including one of those pesky recorders. There were some at the Light who made fun of her for carrying the "suitcase" as they liked to call it, but she found it practical.

Because she mainly covered white-collar crime, most of her stories meant traveling to the upper-class parts of the city. Where she was headed was a far cry from them, but she wasn't worried. Kat always carried a can of mace with her and had found it quite necessary several times. Usually, she'd used it on overzealous fans who seemed to think that just because she was one of the best-known investigative reporters in the city, that gave them the right to try to, not so gently, infuse themselves into her personal life. Kat had also been taking self-defense classes whenever she could for the last five years, so she knew how to handle herself in most situations. It hadn't always been that way.

Since there were few people on the streets, it was relatively quiet, except for the lewd comments made by the city crew working on the water lines. Kat ignored them as she neared the building. When she arrived, she made a note of looking at her watch, and for a brief moment, she thought the cab driver must be psychic. It had taken her exactly fifteen minutes to arrive at the address given to her by the creep on the phone. "This is a waste of time," she told herself again, although her gut still said differently.

Kat retrieved her camera from inside her bag and started taking pictures of the surrounding area. *What a shame.* Less than ten years ago it used to be a highly desirable location for all different sorts of enterprises. From banks that dealt with multinational organizations to brokerage companies, venture capitalists and just about any sphere of interest. But like so many other parts of the city it had fallen prey to the times, as businesses left looking for cheaper rent. What had once been a pristine part of town was now home to buildings that were in varying states of decay. Scattered about were some inhabited by what were probably struggling companies, still clinging to the hope that things would turn around, Kat retriever her camera and took pictures from almost every angle. She didn't want to admit to herself that it was a reason to scan every potential hiding place for the mystery man.

Reluctantly, she turned and faced the building. Kat remembered the pleasure in his voice as he told her that she would find a body inside and she could picture his anticipation of the event. He had called himself "The Chemist." But why? And was he the killer? What kind of trap could she be walking into? But she wasn't one to let anything get in the way of a story. *If there was a story*, she reminded herself.

The front doors were located under a tattered green awning barely attached to the metal frame holding it in place. It whipped around in the breeze making snapping sounds that to her ears seemed menacing, like the sound a bullwhip made when it hit its target. Kat felt thrust forward because of the force of the wind tunnel, caused by the aerodynamics found with tall buildings that stood close together. She heard the crunch of broken glass beneath her feet, looked down and saw it everywhere. The source was the front doors, now covered with sheets of plywood that, given how crooked they were, looked like they had hastily been attached. As edgy as she was, she wondered if whoever had hung them had been in a hurry because they found the building as foreboding as she did. *Fuck this nonsense; I've got a job to do.*

Kat reached for one of the handles and somehow knew the door would be unlocked. He wouldn't have called her if he hadn't wanted her to see what was inside. She was right; it opened with ease. Not that she would have ever admitted it, but she was hoping it wouldn't, leaving her with no choice but to call the police. After Kat retrieved a small flashlight from her bag, she looked for a light switch. Since the building had been vacant for a while, there shouldn't have been any power, but her instinct once again told her that he would have ensured there were no obstacles. Kat located a set of switches just inside the entrance and flipped them all on. Fluorescent lights brightly shone overhead, and she could see most of the first floor of the ten-story building.

The interior of the building looked like a continuation of the exterior—it was just as bleak in appearance. Left behind, presumably by its previous tenant, were one gray, metal desk that tilted to the right because it was missing a leg, and some well-worn chairs that looked haphazardly scattered about as if someone had left in a hurry. For convenience, she had it slung over her shoulder. After she was satisfied that the area was well documented by snapshots, she took a long look at what was in front of her. Kat's imagination was working overtime, and she visualized the space divided into tiny cubicles where drone workers spent their time watching the clock, waiting for their day to be over. She found that image drearier than the interior's current rundown appearance.

Judging by the number of phone lines, it could have been a call center. *Probably a shady one*, Kat surmised. Then, she noticed that one of the chairs was facing towards her and it didn't look like it had aimlessly been left behind like the others. In fact, it looked like it had been deliberately placed in the middle of the cement floor. It was difficult to tell, but there appeared to be someone sitting in it. Even though she wasn't certain what she faced, a sense of dread encompassed her, and she thought she could feel it constricting her lungs so she couldn't breathe. Kat instinctively gasped for air, until in a moment of clarity she realized she was behaving irrationally. After composing herself, she forced the reporter in her to take over. She chastised herself, angry and determined not to let it happen again. *I'm a seasoned veteran, not some silly schoolgirl.*

"Hello, I'm Katherine Hope from the New York Light. Are you the person that called me?" she yelled in vain.

Several of the overhead lights in that location were out, and Kat found the whole scene ominous. She didn't believe in coincidences, yet there they were. All dead. The closer she got, even with the lack of illumination, she thought she could make out long hair and, by the shape of the body, she was sure it was a woman. But she appeared to be slouched in the chair. As cautiously as she could, Kat approached her.

The thought that he lured her there for a reason and that she might wind up like the woman crossed her mind. She fiercely pushed it aside. But, no matter how hard she tried, she couldn't stop her next thought—that she would wind up in the obituaries, all because she couldn't pass up a lead she shouldn't have taken. Perhaps it was a way of escaping what she knew was coming next, but instead of feeling a sense of foreboding, she was surprised to find the whole idea amusing. Since she had no close family, there would only be her co-workers grieving. And, of course, thirty minutes after the news of her death was announced they would turn into buzzards, fighting over her coveted desk near Jimmy's office and then taking off with her office supplies. If Kat was anything, she was a realist. Then her thoughts turned back to what was in front of her, and there was nothing humorous about it.

When Kat reached the chair, she hesitated. She had not seen that many bodies before. But once again she gathered her wits, turned her flashlight on and shone its bright light on the woman. Startled, she jumped backwards and then froze. Kat had never seen anything so gruesome. Even the mangled bodies she had glimpsed in a horrific car accident paled in comparison. Her reporter instinct took over, and Kat quickly regained her composure. She knew that this could be the beginning of a much bigger story, and she had been chosen to cover it by the man who she knew as The Chemist. She could think about what it all meant to her career later because now she had things to do. Fortunately, Kat wasn't squeamish at all.

As an investigative reporter, Kat had learned a lot about crime scenes, but not this kind. Fortunately, she had watched enough CSI on television to know how to approach it. She knew better than to take a chance of contaminating the area so she took pictures from every angle, especially of the woman's face, although she knew she would never need a reminder of it. Her face was contorted into a gruesome death mask. Judging by her look of anguish, whatever the cause of death, it had been excruciating. What had she gotten herself into? Who was this man that had reached out to her, wanting her to see this sickness? Then she thought of something worse. Like a spider he had lured her into his web—would he ever let her go?

Kat decided to call Jimmy, and after she was finally able to get through, she quickly filled him in on the details.

"I don't like it, Kat. What on earth were you thinking? You investigate white-collar crimes, remember? I'll turn it over to Jack. He's used to covering the murders that happen in the city. Get out of there now and call 911," Jimmy told her, sounding worried.

"We don't know that the man who called me is the killer, and even if he is, he had plenty of opportunities to hurt me. I want this story."

"That's how reporters get themselves killed, damn it. Go ahead and cover this case but bury it and don't respond if he calls again. Forward it to Jack so he can follow up."

"And what if that pisses him off and he decides to come after me? No, my best bet is to cover the story and work with the police to catch the person responsible."

"Kat—."

"No, Jimmy. You know I'm smart and careful. Let me follow through."

"Alright. But you notify me immediately if he calls again. And if anything he says or does causes even one hair to stand up. You hear me?"

"Of course."

"Then hang up and call 911 and cooperate fully."

"But you know as well as I do they'll take over the crime scene and try to shut me out."

"Let them."

"Can you at least have someone run down this address and

find out a way to locate the owner?"

"Sure, what is it?"

She told him.

"I'll put Cindy on it right away and have her get back to you as soon as she knows something."

"Okay, I'll make the call." Kat looked at her watch—it was noon.

"911 what is your emergency?"

"I'd like to report a murder."

CHAPTER TWO

IDIOT BOX?

Kat watched as a Ford Interceptor, New York City's cruiser of choice, pulled-up with light flashing and siren wailing. The sound echoed throughout the empty structure, making it seem even louder. Fortunately, it was turned off almost immediately since it had served its purpose but the bothersome light was left on, and the flashing red made the scene seem even more macabre.

One of the police officers quickly approached Kat while the other approached the body and checked for a pulse, to see if there was any way the poor woman could be alive. "Did you see anyone else?"

Kat had gotten out her notepad and written down everything that had happened in her form of short-hand. After reading the officer's name tag, she wrote that down also. She had watched every move the officers made so far, knowing even the smallest thing could turn out to be pertinent. Kat was always thorough.

"No, there was no one that I saw." Kat didn't tell them that the creep was supposed to be watching.

He thanked her then looked at his partner who shook his head indicating the woman was dead. Although it was mostly open space, there were doors in the back, and the officers approached them cautiously. Then, guns in hand, they disappeared from her view, and she knew they were checking out the building and looking for other exits.

Another car arrived, and one of the other officers approached the body, got out his notepad and, as he looked around, like Kat, he took notes. He started taking pictures using the camera he had brought with him. The remaining officer approached her, notebook and pen in hand. His nametag read Gutierrez.

"Are you the one that found the body, ma'am?"

"Yes, I am."

"And you're positive that you saw no one else?"

"There was no one here that I'm aware of."

"Your name is?"

"Katherine Hope."

"Can you describe how you discovered the body?"

"I'm only talking to the lead detective on the case."

"And why is that?"

"That's between the detective and me."

"I'm not sure who the case has been assigned to, but I'll let the detectives know when they arrive."

Kat waited and watched as the Crime Scene Unit arrived. The lead member of the team, a man who appeared quite proficient at his job, examined the body. From watching too many crime shows she knew he was trying to establish cause and time of death. She watched as two men meticulously collected samples of everything around and on the woman's body. From what she saw, it looked like they didn't find much. Kat wasn't surprised; she had a feeling the killer was too smart to leave any evidence behind.

One of the technicians used a digital fingerprinting device in an attempt to identify the woman. Kat saw him write something down, presumably the victim's name. More cars arrived, and she knew they would be canvassing the area looking for potential witnesses. She also knew they would take pictures of the crowd she could see gathering through the open front doors, in case the murderer returned to the scene of the crime. There were two uniformed police officer's questioning those outside.

Next, Kat watched as a plain car arrived, and two men got out. She immediately recognized them as police detectives, easily identifiable because of the cheap looking suits they were wearing. One of the officers spoke to them, and together they walked to the crime scene with the officer talking, and occasionally interrupted by the taller man. Then the officer pointed at her, and both men looked in her direction. They said something to each other, and the detective that had done most of the talking walked towards her while the other, presumably his partner, stayed behind to talk to those working the scene. The detective had a no-nonsense look about him, and she could tell he was sizing her up. But she was busy scrutinizing him. Good-looking, he had the typical professional haircut that didn't manage to stop his hair from being unruly. He was looking at her so intensely she felt like he was dissecting her and that made her uncomfortable. But then she realized that was his objective. His demeanor suggested he was a man who was not one to quit until he got what he wanted. But she was known for her ferociousness and decided that she must immediately get the upper hand. *This is my story, damn it!*

"Katherine Hope?"

"Katherine Hope, investigative reporter for The New York Light," she informed him. Her way of letting him know that she was working and meant business.

"I'm Detective Russo. I understand you refused to talk to anyone but the lead detective."

"That's correct. I don't like wasting my time."

"Nobody does so I hope you're not wasting mine."

"Are you the lead detective?"

"I am."

"Then, you don't have anything to worry about."

"Once again, why did you ask for me?"

"Because I need someone in charge that can negotiate. And

because it's my story and I want to keep it."

"That's not my concern. All I care about is finding out as much as you know about what happened."

"And I care about my job. I'll provide you with as much information as I can in exchange for an exclusive."

"No deal, but you're going to answer my questions anyway."

"There's one important fact you should know."

"And what might that be?"

"You need me. A man called me at work and told me where to find the body."

He hollered at one of the uniformed officers. "Officer Jones, would you take Ms. Hope to the precinct and put her in an interrogation room?"

"Sure thing, Detective," Officer Jones said as he quickly walked towards them. Once he reached where they were standing, he politely asked Kat, "Would you mind coming with me Ms.?"

Looking cool and collected, Kat responded, "No problem, officer."

It wasn't the first time she had been in the back of a police car. She didn't expect it to be her last. When they arrived at the precinct, Officer Jones took her to the third floor and put her in interrogation room two.

"Is there anything I can get you, Miss?" he asked.

"Yes, a large vanilla cappuccino, with non-fat milk and artificial sweetener. I have to watch my figure," Kat added sarcastically.

He returned a few minutes later with a cup of coffee that looked like it had been brewed first thing that morning. It was 1:30 in the afternoon. Kat didn't say a word and took a sip of coffee. It took everything she had to keep from spitting it out. Instead, she looked at the Officer and smiled.

"Delicious."

He shrugged, then left her sitting at the table.

Detective Russo made her wait over an hour, and by then Kat was in an irritable mood. He finally walked in and sat across the table from her, then placed a digital recorder between them. Kat looked at her phone. It was now almost 3 p.m.

"Why did you call 911 and report a murder? The cause of death has yet to be determined."

"What? No foreplay, Detective?" Kat asked coolly.

"Let me repeat myself. Why did you report a murder? Unless you're the perpetrator, how could you know?"

Kat laughed. "I'm an investigative reporter. I received a call from a man who told me where the body was."

"So you say. But if this man only gave you the location, why call it in a murder?" The detective said it slowly as if he were talking to someone too stupid to understand. Kat made a point of showing that it didn't bother her.

"Obviously you weren't at the same crime scene I was."

Detective Russo stared at her as if he were trying to ascertain whether she was telling the truth or not.

"Fine. I could always lawyer up, and then you wouldn't get anything from me," Kat told him with resolve.

"If that's what you want to do."

"You don't want me to do that so let's not play games. I told you, I'll cooperate if you give me an exclusive for the story."

"No deal."

"Might I remind you that the man chose to call me?"

"And why would he do that?"

"Because I'm a damned good reporter."

"I'm familiar with your work," he said with a scowl.

"Not a fan, I take it." He ignored her statement which she took as a "No."

"As I said, he gave me the location of the body, and I decided to check it out before calling the police."

"You called 911 at 12:01 p.m. What time did you arrive at the scene?"

"About 15 minutes earlier."

"And what did you do during that time?"

"I checked to see if he was telling the truth. I went looking for a body."

"Why didn't you call 911 and report it instead of taking a chance?"

"Do you have any idea how many prank calls I get every day?"

He just stared at her.

"I'll take that as a no. I get a lot."

"If you believed it was just a crank-call why did you go there? It's not exactly like that building is near your office."

"Because my gut told me it was worth checking out."

"So, a man who conveniently knows the location of a dead woman calls you and you decide to investigate because of a gut feeling?"

"I already told you the answer to that question."

"Ms. Hope, you're trying my patience."

"I imagine that's not difficult to do."

"Fine. I'll let you call your lawyer. Then I'll call Robert Johnson from The Beacon and give him the story."

"No, you won't. You're going to give me an exclusive."

"What makes you so sure?"

Kat just confidently smiled at him.

"You're free to go."

"You need me, and you know it. I told you, let's not waste each other's time."

"You have a rather high opinion of yourself."

"Yes, but it's well-deserved."

"Fine, I'll check with my captain."

"I knew you'd see it my way."

That provoked a response from him. "You think this is funny? A young woman is dead, and you're making wise-cracks."

"No, I don't think it's funny. What I do find funny is all the time we've wasted for you to agree to give me what you knew you had to give me the second I told you I had received the call from that man. Now be a good boy and go talk to your Captain."

"Fine," he responded, looking disgusted.

"You know where to find me."

Detective Russo left without another word. Fifteen minutes later he returned.

"The captain agreed."

"Good. Now we're getting somewhere."

"We'll see. Now tell me exactly what he said."

"He asked me if I was Katherine Hope, the reporter that did the story on Steven Garrett."

"Yes, I remember that story. You helped a mobster, who was probably responsible for multiple deaths, go free."

"I only report the facts, Detective."

He scowled at her again and looked like he wanted to say something but refrained.

"What next?"

"I told him I was. He informed me that he had chosen me because he knew I would take him seriously. Then he told me the address and that I would find a woman's body there but to come alone and that he would be watching.

"Can you describe his voice?"

Kat was prepared. "Caucasian, late 20's to early 30's, no accent of any kind. But it was his tone that stood out."

"How so?"

"He seemed pleased with himself."

"And you never considered that it might be a trap?"

"Of course I did. But I'm pretty good at taking care of myself."

"Is that so? Good enough to take on a man who is connected somehow to the death of a young woman?"

"He never said he was the killer."

"Then why did you say, 'I want to report a murder'?"

"Because it looked like one."

"So now you're an expert on the cause of death? If it turns out she died of natural causes or was a suicide you could be charged with making a false police report."

"That's bullshit. That scene was staged. And that poor woman's face? Did that look like anything you'd ever seen before? Maybe I should ask for a real detective."

"I'm afraid you're stuck with me. Now can we continue? Let's go back to why you decided to go in the first place."

"I wasn't sure what I'd find. Like I told you already I get lots of—"

"Crank calls."

"Exactly."

"Would you recognize his voice if you heard it again?"

"I believe so. Have you identified the body yet?" Kat asked as she retrieved her notepad and a pen.

"When do you plan on running this story?"

"I'd like to get it this evening's edition if I can get out of here on time," she added sarcastically.

"We're still trying to track down her next of kin."

"I can save that information until you have. What was the cause of death?"

"You squeamish?"

"No. After what I saw and the fact that I remained calm, why would you ask?"

"Then let's take a trip to the morgue."

Kat grabbed her bag. "I'm ready."

"We'll see." It was 4:00 p.m.

CHAPTER THREE

DEATH DELIGHTS

They drove to the city morgue in Detective Russo's unmarked Chevy Impala. The morgue was located in the basement of the building on First Avenue near 32nd Street, just underneath the pavement of the East Side of the city. As they got out of his car, Kat noticed that it was still warm for that time of year. She looked up and noticed that the leaves of the trees that lined the street were changing colors, about the only thing consistent with the fall weather. As they entered the City Morgue the first thing Kat noticed was the sign hanging in the lobby: "Let conversation cease, let laughter flee. This is the place where death delights in helping the living." She didn't know why, but she took out her notebook and paused to write it down.

"You coming or not?"

"Of course."

Detective Russo knew exactly where he was going because there was no hesitation on his part. Down the stairs, they went where they reached a long hallway. As they walked towards the end of it, Kat could swear she heard the low whispers of the dead as they tried to tell her their story. She had an irrational thought. *Maybe they know I'm a reporter and want me to listen.* She managed to gather her wits and shut out the imagined, unwelcome sounds. Then, she noticed the smell—it was pungent and made her throat and nostrils feel irritated. She turned to Detective Russo, "For God's sake, what is that horrible smell?"

He looked at her and smiled. "It's formaldehyde. After a while you barely even notice it. But others probably will, so I suggest you change clothes afterwards." Great, that meant stopping by the apartment. Not that she had time. Kat thought about what he said about getting used to the smell but decided that wouldn't happen because she didn't plan on going there again. At least, that's what she hoped.

In a harshly lit room was a man in a white lab coat, standing over a body doing something that made a distinctive, loud, snapping sound. Kat knew she didn't want to see what was causing the sound that emanated from the body but forced herself not to look away. He was using something that looked like hedge snippers to cut through the body's ribs. There was something about the procedure that caused her to stare out of morbid curiosity. Kat managed to tear her eyes away long enough to look around the room. There were eight steel tables, some large containers with chemicals and shelves lined with plastic containers. She reminded herself to ask Detective Russo about them after they left.

The first thing the man said when he saw Detective Russo was, "You here about the female that just came in, Dante? Cause if you are I haven't gotten to her yet. I've got a backlog, and I'm busy." Then he noticed Kat. "Aren't you going to introduce me?"

"Murph, this is Katherine Hope from the New York Light. Ms. Hope this is Medical Examiner, David Murphy."

"But you can call me Murph," the medical examiner added.

"Can you guess as to cause of death?" asked Dante.

"You know better than to ask that."

"Come on, Murph."

"Fine, I'll take a look at her." He went to a drawer and pulled out a sliding tray. On it was the body of the young woman. He pulled the sheet back and started examining her. "No signs of blunt force trauma that I can find, but I'll need to do further examination before I can rule it out. No ligature marks so we can rule out stran-gulations." Then he lifted one arm and stared at it intently then looked at her other arm and pointed to the inside of her forearm. "See these track marks? It could be a simple drug overdose," he said, sounding disinterested.

"What about poison?"

"Could be that too, but I won't know more until I perform the autopsy. But if I find a high level of drugs in her bloodstream, it could mask a lot of poisons so it could be practically impossible to tell. Depending on the poison. If she was poisoned," Murphy added, sounding doubtful.

"What if I told you that Ms. Hope received a tip from a man who claimed the woman was killed with poison and told her where to locate the body?"

"Alright, you made your point. I'll perform an autopsy on her as soon as I'm done with him," Murphy said, as he pointed towards the body on the table.

"What do you have as the time of death?"

"Approximately 9:30 a.m. Today. One other thing. Based on lividity her body was moved after she was dead."

"Good to know. Keep me informed?"

"Of course."

"Okay. Thanks, Murph." Then he turned to Kat. "I'd like to put a listening device on your phone."

She thought for a moment, uncertain. "I'll have to talk to Jimmy."

"Alright then. Here's what you're going to write."

"You can't dictate that!"

"You want to catch this guy or not?"

"But we don't even know if he killed her."

"He knows enough and wants attention, or he wouldn't have called you. Write your story but list her as being unidentified and then bury it."

"Detective this could be front page news."

"Not anymore, it's not."

Kat went to see Jimmy. "Detective Russo wants to bug my phone, in hopes of catching The Chemist."

"Absolutely not. What if it got out? Do you think you get any more tips from confidential sources?"

He also wants me to bury the story about the murder victim in hopes of drawing The Chemist out."

"I don't like it."

"But what if he's right?"

"We're not here to help the police solve crimes. We're here to report them."

"But Jimmy—"

"Fine. Do what you want."

~***~

~By Katherine Hope The New York Light

Woman's body found in an abandoned building in the Bronx

October 2nd

An unidentified woman's body was found around 12:15 this afternoon. Cause of death has yet to be determined. She is described as Caucasian, approximately 23 years old, with long blonde hair, green eyes, weight 127 lbs. and 5' 7". If you know of anyone that is missing fitting that description, call the 13th Precinct at (212)555-1247.

~***~

"Detective Russo. I hope you're happy. My editor nearly had a heart attack when I told him what I was doing."

"Just be sure to tell me when, or should I say if, you hear from him." Kat still hadn't told Detective Russo what the killer had referred to himself.

"I'll hear from him again. And you'll be the first to know," Kat lied.

"Why do I doubt you, Ms. Hope?"

"Because you're a cynic?"

"Or maybe because after all my years of experience I've become a good judge of character."

"Isn't that the same thing?"

"Goodbye, Ms. Hope." And with that, he hung up before she could ask him some questions. She called him right back.

"Detective Russo we had a deal. You're supposed to keep me apprised of developments in the case."

"What do you want to know?"

"To start with, what's her name?"

"Susan Blake."

"And?"

"And what?"

Kat sighed. "You're not going to make this easy, are you?"

"Where have I heard that before?"

"Can you cut the crap, Detective?"

"What do you want to know?"

"How old was she? What was her background? I need to know if she was married or had a boyfriend, her immediate family member's names, if she worked and where, had she filed any complaints against anyone for stalking her or for harassment, and did she have a record. You get the drift."

"She was 23, wasn't married, but had a boyfriend of two years, Mark Redford, 27. He's a stockbroker who works for Portal Investment. Her immediate family members are her father, Judge Richard Blake, her mother, Jillian Blake, artist, and younger brother, Joseph, a Junior at NYU. She worked at her mother's gallery, Trend Art Studios after she graduated with a Bachelor of Arts at New York Art Institute two years ago. No complaints of any kind were filed, and her record was clean except for a drug charge. She was busted for having a couple of joints in her junior year. The charges were dropped."

"Let me guess; her Dad had something to do with that."

"That would be my guess also."

"Any forensic evidence?"

"They're still processing it."

"In other words, you have nothing."

"So far."

"And the cause of death?"

"The Medical Examiner found cocaine in her system but no sign of poison."

"So, it's not being ruled as a homicide?"

"Foul play hasn't been ruled out."

"I'd hope not. I believe the call I received was genuine."

"We're bringing in the boyfriend for questioning.

"You don't think he was behind this, do you?"

"I'm exploring all avenues."

"Can I watch when you question him?"

"Of course, you have an exclusive, remember?"

Kat smiled. "I'm glad I didn't have to remind you."

"I'd like some more time to convince my Captain to treat it as a homicide."

"How do you intend to do that?"

"I need another day."

"And I need time to conduct interviews. But I need to print something in tonight's edition."

"You want your story or not?"

"Of course."

"Then give me a day."

Kat hesitated, “Fine.”

“Thank you, Ms. Hope.”

“Besides, as I said, I have interviews to conduct.”

“If you think you’re going to question her parents you’re wasting your time.”

“I told you, I’m good at my job.”

“I believe you, Ms. Hope.”

“For the love of God, call me Kat.”

“Yes, Ms. Hope. And you can call me Detective Russo.”

“Goodbye, Dante.” It was 5:30 p.m.

CHAPTER FOUR

HOME, SWEET, HOME

As Detective Russo had warned her, Kat's attempts at interviews went nowhere. The Blake's were not talking, all questions were directed to their lawyer who simply stated that the family wished to mourn in private. Susan's boyfriend was in hiding, and no one was saying where. Her brother was at the family's mansion. She called the art gallery only to get a message that they were closed.

Since it was too late, and the office would be closed, she decided to go to the New York Art Institute the following morning. Kat called a taxi to take her home. Then, she realized she forgot to ask Detective Russo about the plastic containers in the morgue. Even though it wasn't relevant to the story, she was curious.

Kat's apartment, unlike the rest of her life as a reporter, was very tidy and had been carefully decorated. Being a journalist didn't pay a lot, but she spent her money wisely, and along with her ability to sew, she managed to pull off a look that was very warm and inviting. She loved her apartment and always thought of it as a refuge at the end of the day. That evening was no different.

After the day she'd had, she was too tired to cook, so she checked her refrigerator and found enough leftovers for a decent meal. While she heated up her dinner, she set the table. Kat loved fresh flowers, and it was the one thing she splurged on and always had a centerpiece for her dining room table. After the microwave timer went off, she took the plate and set it on the placemat and then poured herself a glass of red wine. She went to sit down, and that was when she noticed a piece of paper under the vase. It sent a chill up her spine because she knew that the sanctity of her home had been violated.

Kat called Detective Russo because she didn't know who else to call and told him what she found. He told her to go to a neighbor's apartment then asked for the number. She gave him Mrs. Watson's.

As if he could still hear her, she said out loud, "How do you know where I live?" Kat decided she would have to find out, but at the moment there were more important concerns. She quickly went across the hall and knocked on Mrs. Watson's door. Even though she was a widow she still preferred to be called Mrs. Since Kat had never seen her go anywhere, she knew she had to be home. A few moments later, she heard Mrs. Watson approach the door and then stop. *She's looking through the peephole.* Then Kat heard her unlock the door and the sound of the chain as she removed it from the slide that held it in place.

The door opened, and Mrs. Watson seemed delighted to have a visitor.

"Kat. It's so good to see you. Come in."

"Thank you, Mrs. Watson," she said, then quickly entered her apartment.

"I'm sorry to bother you, but I'll only be here a moment."

"Is something wrong?"

Then it occurred to her. Mrs. Watson was known as somewhat of a busybody because she always knew what took place on the 2nd floor.

"You didn't happen to see a man go in my apartment today, did you?"

"Why yes, I did. It was about two hours ago, and I heard

someone, and I thought—"

The buzzer went off, "Hold that thought, Mrs. Watson. I need to let someone in."

Kat pressed the speaker button on the pad next to the door. "Dante?"

"Yes, hurry and buzz me in." A few minutes later she heard knocking and looked through the peephole. It was Dante. Mrs. Watson hadn't locked the door after letting her in, so Kat quickly opened it and gestured for him to come in. Then she noticed Mrs. Watson staring at them and realized how bizarre the situation must seem to her.

"Mrs. Watson, I'd like to introduce De—" she quickly caught herself not wanting to alarm the poor woman. "This is Dante Russo; he's an old friend of the family."

"What a pleasure to meet you, Mr. Russo. Where are my manners? I just made a cherry pie that's still warm from the oven. Could I offer you two a slice?"

"No, thank you," they both said in unison. Kat thought under different circumstances it would have been funny, but there was nothing to laugh about considering what she had found. That thought was so unfathomable to her; she felt as if it were a bad dream from which she couldn't wake up. Especially after everything that had happened.

"Dante, Mrs. Watson was telling me she saw someone go into my apartment two hours ago."

"Is that so? You didn't tell me you were expecting any other company."

"I wasn't. Which is why I was so surprised." Kat turned to the senior woman.

"You said you saw him. Would you mind giving me a description so I can try to figure out who he is? I'd like to give him a call. Since he came over instead of phoning me, it could be important." Kat realized she was rambling, so she stopped talking.

"To be honest, I couldn't get a good look at him. He had on

a baseball cap that was pulled down low and was wearing sunglasses. Plus, he had on a jacket, and the collar was pulled up so I couldn't see his face. I remember thinking how odd it was considering how warm it has been for this time of year."

Kat felt profound disappointment because she had gotten her hopes up for no reason. She wanted nothing more than for this nightmare to end. Then she heard Dante speaking and tried to focus.

"You wouldn't happen to know how tall he was, would you?" Dante asked casually. She didn't know how he could be so calm.

"How tall are you, Dante? Is it okay if I call you that, or do you prefer Mr. Russo?"

He smiled at her, and it was so disarming she could see Mrs. Watson relax.

"Dante is fine, ma'am. I'm six feet, two inches."

"First Dante, please don't call me ma'am. You can call me Delores." Kat stared at Dante. She had lived there five years, and Mrs. Watson had never told Kat what her first name was.

"Yes, Delores. So, how tall would you say he was?" He asked the question so casually they could have been talking about the weather.

"I'd say he was three inches shorter than you, so five eleven. Are you sure there's nothing I could get you?" Before Dante could respond, she leaned in, and Kat could swear she giggled. "Don't tell anyone but I keep beer on hand. Would you like one?"

"How very gracious of you but I have to pass." He gave her that look again before proceeding. "Could you tell how he was built? Was he slender or—"

"Dante, I already told you he was wearing a coat. And I couldn't see below it. These peepholes don't let me see much, unfortunately." She smiled at him as if she wanted nothing more than to please him.

Kat decided to speak up in an attempt to dissuade any suspicion Delores might have when she later thought about the conversation. "That's such a shame. Now I have no idea who it was. Oh," she said as if the thought had just occurred to her. "What about his cap. I have several friends that are sports fans. Did it have a team name or logo?"

She turned to Kat as if she'd forgotten she was there.

"No dear, it didn't have any markings at all. It was just a plain white cap."

Kat tried to look confused and paused for a moment as if she were thinking. Then, pretending the thought had just come to her, she turned to the senior woman.

"I know, did you happen to see what color his hair was?"

"Why I sure did," she responded, obviously pleased with herself. "It was light brown."

"Thanks, Mrs. Watson. I think I know who it might be. You've been very helpful. We better not keep you any longer."

"Oh, but it was my pleasure," she said, looking at Dante.

"The pleasure was all mine, Delores," responded Dante.

They walked out of the apartment together, but before Kat could touch the doorknob, Dante stopped her and pulled a plastic bag out of his pocket and used it to grasp the knob and opened the door.

"Stay outside and don't touch the doorknob. Let me sweep your apartment and make sure it's clear."

Kat could only nod. He returned five minutes later.

"It's clear. Come in and show me the note."

She entered her apartment reluctantly then went to the table.

"It's right there under the vase."

"Did you touch it?"

"Of course not!"

Dante took a pair of gloves out of his jacket and put them on. Then he gently lifted the vase and set it aside. Next, he picked up the piece of paper and read it.

"Tell me what it says."

"Kat dear, I'm very disappointed in how you handled my story. You're very important, or I wouldn't have called you. Don't make me regret it."

"Let me get CSU in here. Maybe he left a clue," said Dante.

"No, that would alarm the neighbors," replied Kat.

"Wouldn't you rather catch him?"

"Yes, but I think he's too smart to leave a clue."

"Why do you say that?"

Kat paused not knowing how to explain. Finally, she said, "Let's call it a gut feeling."

Dante let out an exasperated sigh. "I'll take the note in tomorrow to check anyway. I'm also going to dust the doorknob and the vase. Do you have a make-up brush, cocoa powder, and transparent tape?"

"Yes, let me get them." It didn't take long for Kat to gather the items.

Dante took his time dusting everything but let out an exasperated sigh.

"He wiped everything clean."

"I'm not surprised."

He looked at her with a no-nonsense expression. "I'm spending the night here."

"I'm sure that won't be necessary."

"I insist."

Kat knew she would feel better if he were there, so she agreed. She got out fresh sheets and a pillow and set them on the couch for him.

"I hope this is fine, Detective. There is an extra toothbrush in the bathroom."

"That will work. I think we're past formalities. Call me Dante."

"Call me Kat. Good night Dante."

"I'll be back tomorrow to install a security camera."

"Okay."

He looked at her plate on the table. "Aren't you going to eat your dinner?"

"I'm not hungry anymore." It was 9:30 p.m.

When Kat woke up the next morning, Dante was gone. He had left a note telling her he was going to have the paper analyzed and would let her know if they found anything. Kat was glad it was gone, but she hadn't forgotten what it said.

The first thing she did was go to the Art Institute where she was able to track down a couple of friends of Susan's from when she had been a student there.

One of them confided in her, off the record.

"Susan had a drug problem alright."

"What was she using?"

"She'd try anything, but mostly she used cocaine."

"Do you know who her supplier was?"

"I hate to answer that question. I don't want to get anyone in trouble."

"Don't you want to help catch her killer?"

"Yeah, I do. It was Susan's boyfriend, Mark Redford."

"Thanks, so much."

"Will my name be in the paper?"

"Only if you want it to."

"Definitely not!"

"Then it won't be."

"Thanks."

The owner of the building where Susan's body has been found finally phoned her. "Yes, it was a call center."

"Do you know why the electricity was on?"

"Beats me, I had it turned off. There's no way in hell I want to pay an electric bill for an empty building."

"Would you mind checking to see who authorized it?"

"Not a problem. I'd like to know myself."

Kat was certain whoever it was had used an alias, but she was willing to try anything to gain a clue as to his identity. She was that desperate.

Kat called Dante to see if he had any new information.

"The M.E. still can't find any evidence of poison. He's ruling it as a cocaine overdose."

"He's wrong."

"What are you going to do?"

"I'm going to say she was murdered and the cause of death was poison."

"But, Kat, you have no evidence to corroborate your story."

"Are you forgetting the note?"

Kat hung up. Fifteen minutes later her phone rang.

"Hello, dear."

"I take it you got my note."

"I did."

"If you know what's good for you, you'll write the story as if your life depended on it." The Chemist laughed, and the sound was almost her undoing. She took a deep breath and managed to calm herself.

"I will. Do you mind if I ask you some questions so I can write the story you deserve?" *You cold-hearted bastard.*

"Go ahead. dear"

Kat swallowed hard before she said anything. "Why her?"

"Why not her?"

"I want to write the best story I can. I'd like to know."

"Let's just say she was convenient."

"Was it because of her father?"

The Chemist just laughed, only it didn't sound like a laugh coming from him. It sounded more like the sound you would expect to hear from a monster in a horror movie. It was pure evil.

"How did you kill her?"

"What did I tell you to call me, Kat?" Hearing him call her by her nickname made her shudder. *Why is he obsessed with me?* If she could find that out, maybe she could stop him.

"The Chemist."

"You're smart. I'm sure you can figure it out." He hung up. If The Chemist wasn't the killer, he knew who was.

She hesitated before she called Detective Russo. But she tried to keep her word.

"He just called."

"What did he say?"

"Nothing that helps your case."

"Tell me anyway," he said impatiently.

She relayed the conversation but once again left out the fact that he called himself The Chemist, although she wasn't sure why. Maybe it would reveal that she knew more than they did, and the police would consider her to be invaluable, she told herself.

"He insisted I run the story today and I'm going to."

"Any way I could see an advance copy?"

"It'll be a cold day in hell before that happens."

"That's what I thought you'd say."

"Any comments for the paper?"

"At this point? Just write that I couldn't be reached."

"What about the note? Anything?"

"No, as we suspected, he's too clever."

Then she remembered. "What are the plastic containers in

the

morgue used for?"

"Mostly to store organs." Kat wished she hadn't asked.

The developed photos were waiting for her on her desk. She used a magnifying lens but found nothing that could help. The man that owned the building had run into a dead end when he tried to find out who had paid to have the electricity tuned on.

Finally, she received a call from Dante that they had located the boyfriend Mark Redford, and had brought him in for questioning, and that a squad was waiting out front for her. When they arrived the Sgt. at the desk told her the interrogation room they were in then waved her through. Dante was waiting for her.

"You ready?"

Kat already had her notepad and pen out.

"Yes."

Dante went into the interrogation room and didn't waste any time getting down to business. "Where were you the morning of October 1st."

Redford hesitated. "I was on my way to a meeting."

"What meeting was that?"

"Does this have to do with Susan's death?"

"We're just asking routine questions, to anyone she was close to."

"My ass, I want to see my lawyer."

"Alright, you can make your phone call."

Dante left the interrogation room and met up with Kat.

"Looks like a dead end."

"I'm going to run my story."

~***~

Katherine Hope The New York Light

Unidentified body revealed to be Appellate Court Judge Richard Blake's daughter

October 2nd

Yesterday, it was reported that the body of a young woman was discovered in an abandoned building in the Bronx. Her body was positively identified as Susan Blake, 23, daughter of the Appellate Court Judge, known as Judge Steel because of his reputation for doling out maximum sentences, and her mother Jillian, owner of Trend Art Studios, where Ms. Blake had worked for the past two years. A reliable source stated that Ms. Blake had an ongoing drug problem. According to the Medical Examiner, Dr. David Murphy, cocaine was found in her blood-stream. Yesterday, I received a call from a man who referred to himself as The Chemist who indicated that poison was the cause of death although he would not say what the delivery method was. He did not give a reason as to why Ms. Blake was chosen, although he did not deny she was murdered because of her father's hardline stance on crime. Detective Dante Russo, the lead detective on the case, could not be reached for comment. Readers will be apprised if there are any updates to this case.

~***~

Kat was getting ready to leave to do interviews regarding a fire that had killed a family while they slept. The building was located in Beacon Heights, a well-known area with run-down apartments, infamous for its slum lord, Mike "The King" Wilson. She hoped to get some dirt on him and expose him for what he was. But he proved to be elusive. Kat was expecting a call from Dante as soon as the newspaper hit the stands but tried to concentrate on her story instead of thinking about it.

"Why the hell didn't you tell me he called himself The Chemist?"

"It didn't seem relevant."

"Not relevant my ass. It makes it more likely that the cause of death was poison. And why include the part about the judge? They're a griev-ing family, for God's sake. Have you no compassion?"

"I only report the

news. I don't make it up."

"Does that mean you have to be a cold-hearted bitch to be a good reporter?"

That wasn't the first time she had been called that, so she wasn't offended.

"Sometimes."

"From now on you don't withhold information from me, understand?"

"Yes, sir. One question. How did you know where I live?"

"Goodbye, Ms. Hope." He hung up.

Almost immediately she received another call from The Chemist.

"Very good Kat, dear. I'm impressed. You'll be hearing from me."

CHAPTER FIVE

SLUMMIN' IT

Kat kept herself busy by writing a lengthy feature about the decrease in crime in the city. It took some time to gather the facts. There were several opinions by experts, but she was finally finished, and the article was ready for publication. She was thinking about the Chemist and was worried because the police had no leads on him. Two weeks had passed, and she hoped it was over. Then the phone rang.

"Hello dear."

"What do you want?" He didn't answer her question.

"Go to Cassandra Bay, Complex 12, Apartment 2-4B. And come alone, dear. As usual, I'll be watching so if you try anything I'll know. You know what that means."

The Chemist hung up. She wanted to call Dante but was afraid it would anger The Chemist. That was the last thing she wanted. It was difficult to see a way out.

Kat decided not to tell Jimmy either. She hated that she was breaking her word. He was the closest thing she'd ever had to a father, and she cared about him more than anyone else. She loved him dearly but was afraid to admit that to herself. Life had taught her it was dangerous to get attached. But he had been there when she needed someone to help her. Her head felt like it was swirling. What could she do? Jimmy would never allow her to go anywhere that was dangerous. "Never again," he had told her. Never would he let anyone hurt her, he had promised. *Oh, Jimmy.*

It took three tries before she found a cab driver that would take her to that location, even when she offered to pay double.

"I'll drop you off there lady, but after that, you're on your own. I don't got a death wish."

"That'll be fine." Cassandra Bay had a reputation for being the worst neighborhood in New York City. If that's what you wanted to call it. There was nothing but run-down apartment buildings inhabited by gangs, drug dealers and criminals of all kinds. Unfortunately, lost in the mix were families that couldn't afford anything better.

Once they reached the address The Chemist had given her she paid the cabbie who promptly took off. After looking around, she didn't blame him. Usually self-confident in her ability to take care of herself, she felt unnerved by the hostile faces that seemed to be everywhere. And they were all staring at her. Trying to act as if she belonged, she started to walk up the steps leading to the entrance of the building, only to have her way blocked.

"What do you want, bitch?" one of the men said. The voice came from behind her. Kat slowly turned around and faced him. He couldn't have been more than twenty, but he proudly sported the gang tattoo of The Razors. They were well-known for encroaching on other gang's territories to expand theirs and also proudly displayed markings depicting the number of people they killed. He had five. Kat was good at thinking on her feet, and she knew that her life was on the line, so she'd better think fast.

"My name is Katherine Hope, and I'm a reporter for the Light. I received a call from a woman in this building asking me to write a story about the terrible conditions here."

"You lying, bitch. Ain't nobody fool enough to set foot here, especially someone claiming to be a fancy reporter."

"I can prove who I am if you'll let me show you my credentials."

"Don you go and try to make me look the fool by using them big ass words."

"B, why you wastin' time talking to this fine pussy? Let's have fun then cap her."

"Shut the fuck up. I'm doin' the talkin'."

"Let me just reach inside my bag and I'll prove who I am," Kat told him, calmly. But she felt anything but calm.

"You do dat. Don't be tryin' nothin'."

"I won't." Kat carefully reached inside her bag and pulled out her press badge and showed it to him.

"What she call herself?"

"She didn't give me her name because she was afraid of what would happen to her. All she gave me was her address. Her apartment number is 2-4B."

"That's ole Ms. Nelly's apartment. She been plaining bout this place for years. A'ight bitch, follow me."

The crowd parted way for him without a word. Kat followed him up two flights of stairs. The building walls were covered with graffiti and Kat saw a rat scurrying down the hall when they got to the second floor. They reached apartment 4B, and he knocked on the door.

"Ms. Nelly? It's Jake. Theys, a reporter, wants to talk to ya." No response. Then he tried the knob, and the door was unlocked. "Ms. Nelly?" Then they both saw the body at the same time. Sitting tied to a chair, but slumped over the dining room table, was a blonde woman with long hair. *At least now we know he has a type.*

"What da fuck?" Jake said as he looked at her. Kat looked at him as if she were surprised.

"Don't touch her, Jake. We need to let the police investigate."

"Fuck da shit. We gonna dump the body. If you know what's good for ya, you'll get da fuck outta here."

Kat left and waited until she was away from the building to call Dante. She told him where she was and what was going on.

"Are you crazy? You could have been killed."

"He told me he would be watching, and to come alone. I had no choice."

"Like hell! I'll send a unit to get you right away."

"I don't think that's a good idea. Can you come to get me?"

"I'm on my way."

After he picked her up, he put out a call for all units to go to the crime scene. He dropped Kat off in a safe area and waited until she got in a cab.

When Kat got back to the newspaper, she knew she had to tell Jimmy. She went to see him, but when she went to open her mouth, she lost it. He took her in his arms and tried to soothe her. When she finally calmed down, she told him everything.

"Kat, what were you thinking? You could have been killed."

She smiled at him hoping he would take it as a sign that she was okay. But she wasn't. "That's the first thing Dante said."

"Who the hell is Dante?" Jimmy roared.

"Calm down. He's the lead detective on the case. His last name is Russo."

"You should have told me about him right away. Are you seeing each other?" His voice was so full of concern she thought her heart would break. Then she caught herself.

"No, Jimmy. It's nothing like that. He's just been very helpful to me."

"And that puts you on a first name basis with him?"

"Jimmy, do I have to remind you that I'm a grown woman? Adults usually call each other by their first name, or have you forgotten that?"

"I just want you to be careful. But I'm pulling you off the story and I'm hiring a bodyguard."

"No. You're overreacting. And you know as well as I do that he won't talk to anyone else."

"Who cares? You are not investigating this kind of story anymore. It's just too dangerous. I'm sure you have other stories you can write about."

"Jimmy, I appreciate that you care but I don't think I have a choice.

I'm afraid if I stop he'll come after me. And don't tell me that I'll be safe because you're going to hire a bodyguard. This man is too smart and dangerous. He killed someone and we can't even find proof of how he did it. And he placed a body in the middle of Cassandra Bay. He'll kill anyone that gets in his way. She knew that was true and it scared her. Kat wanted nothing more than to write about the kind of stories she was used to. The kind that didn't get you killed.

"I don't like this Kat. At least come stay with me and Marge until this is over. Do the police really have some good leads?"

Kat knew she had to lie to him again but she felt she didn't have a choice. He would never allow her to continue with this story.

"Yes, they do. I'm sure this will all be over soon. If anyone can catch him it's Detective Russo and I'm certain he will as quickly as possible."

Jimmy sighed and she hated the way he looked at her. "Just be careful, Kat. If you won't do it for yourself do it for me. I love you kid-do, and you're part of my family. And families look out for each other. Remember that, okay?"

"I will, Jimmy."

Dante called her two hours after she returned to her desk.

"It looks like she was killed with the same way Susan Blake was killed. We have a name for her but it turned out to be fake and since she had no forms of identification on her we'll have to keep looking. I don't know what else to tell you, Kat."

"What was the scene like when the police officers arrived?"

"Very hostile. Several gang members pulled guns out but one of the officers was able to calm them down."

"What was his name?"

"Officer Adam Moore."

"What did she look like and do you have any distinguishing features, height, weight, etc.?"

"She has long blonde hair that stops midway down her back, green eyes, approximately five seven, 130 lbs. Nothing distinguishing that we could see but we won't know more until the Medical Examiner performs an autopsy. The only thing we really learned was that he has a type. But let's keep that off the record." *Tell me something I don't know.*

"I wonder how The Chemist got in that building to plant the body? According to the description he's Caucasian and would stand out.

"We thought about that, too."

"And?"

"It doesn't fit what little information Mrs. Watson gave us. But he could have an accomplice."

"What about the occupant of the apartment? Ms. Nelly."

"We found her unconscious in a closet. She didn't remember anything, and the poor woman was so frightened she could barely talk. Leave her name out of the paper, would you?" Dante said, with great frustration.

"I don't plan on it. The poor old woman has been through enough."

"What did your boss say?"

"He wants to pull me off the story and hire a bodyguard."

"You should listen to him."

"You know I can't do that."

"Regardless, I'm going to make it a priority to keep tabs on you." Kat could tell he cared but it frightened her. *Why do people keep acting that way?*

Kat sighed. "Any official statement?"

"We have new leads that we are pursuing."

"Alright. I have enough to write a story. I just wish I didn't have to write about these murders anymore."

"Me too."

~***~

Katherine Hope The New York Light

Unidentified woman's body found in Cassandra Bay

October 16th

The body of another victim was found in an apartment in Cassandra Bay this morning, after the man who calls himself The Chemist called in a tip as to her location.

The scene was tense as police officers arrived only to be confronted by armed members of the gang known as the Razors. Officer Adam Moore, of the 19th Precinct, was able to diffuse the situation so that investigators could process the crime scene. The victim is a Caucasian female with blonde hair that goes midway down her back. She has green eyes, is 5'7" tall and weighs approximately 130 lbs. If you have any information regarding the identity of the deceased woman call (212)555-1257. Detective Dante Russo, lead investigator of the case, stated the following: "The New York City Police Department has obtained several clues and is narrowing down in on their search for the man that refers to himself as The Chemist."

~***~

Dante called. "I just saw the article. If it were only true we have more than two leads, the little bit of description Mrs. Watson gave us and that he likes blondes. But don't print that or it will cause panic."

"I won't. But at least we do have a partial description. Besides, I thought I'd try and see if I could make him sweat."

"I have a feeling this guy doesn't sweat."

Kat let out a deep sigh. "Me either."

"Promise me you won't go to any more crime scenes on your own."

"After almost getting killed yesterday I don't even have to think about making that promise."

"I'm glad to hear that."

"Now I have a promise I want you to make."

"What's that?"

"You'll stop keeping tabs on me."

"I'm only concerned for your safety. This guy means business and I don't want you to wind up next."

"How touching," she responded nonchalantly. "But what do you think it'll do to my reputation as a reporter if someone finds out I have a police detective tailing me?"

"What will your reputation matter if you wind up dead?"

"In a cheery mood today, I see."

"There hasn't been anything to cheer about lately. I promise I'll be a barrel cop of laughs once we catch this monster."

Kat laughed. "I can't imagine you ever being that way. You're always so serious."

"Hazard of the job, I guess."

"I imagine that's true for any homicide detective. But don't let the job ruin your life."

"Words of advice from a woman who went into the most notorious part of the city today all alone?"

"If you had been with me they would have made you as a cop right away and we'd both be dead."

"I wouldn't have gone there with you alone. I'd have had every available unit in the police department with me."

"Even with the response the police got today? There could have been a lot of casualties today—on both sides."

"That's a chance every officer on the force is supposed to be willing to take."

"Well, I've had as much morbid talk as I can take today. I need to wait and see if he calls."

"You know the drill."

"Yes, Detective."

"One other thing. I placed a camera in your hallway facing your door. If he comes back again hopefully we'll be able to tell more."

They hung up. She sat there thinking about his concern for her and didn't realize she was smiling until she heard Amanda, one of the Metro Reporters say, "It's good to see you smiling again, Kat."

"Oh, hi, Amanda. Thank you." Just then the phone rang. Expecting it to be him, she answered coolly.

"I think I know who the dead girl is," she heard a young man's voice say.

"What's your name?"

"Never mind that. Her name is Mary Monroe and she lived in the dorms at NYU"

"But how—"

He hung up. She called Dante.

"Did he call?"

"No, a young man called. He said her name is Mary Monroe and that she goes to NYU."

"Thanks, Kat, I'll check into it. Let me know if he calls again."

"I will."

Two hours later the phone rang. It was Dante.

"The dead woman was positively identified as Mary Monroe, age 20, and a sophomore and NYU. Guess who her father is?"

"I'm not in the guessing mood."

"Senator Charles Monroe."

"Then I need to see if I can get an interview."

"Not likely. He didn't even want to talk to us and doesn't want her name in the paper. Anyway, the guy that called you was him?"

"Definitely not. If I had to guess I'd say he went to school with her."

"Why do you say that?"

"Because he sounded very young and the way he said her name. It suggested some form of intimacy."

"Like a boyfriend?"

"Or someone that was infatuated with her."

"Okay, that was very helpful. I'll talk to you later."

Kat went to NYU and interviewed Mary's roommate and several others that knew her. They all said that she was a cocaine user. She called Dante.

"Why the hell didn't you tell me she used cocaine?"

"The Senator didn't want it in the papers and I had orders not to release that information from the Chief of Police."

"Why the alias?"

"We had a hard time finding out but apparently she had a stalker."

"Next time honor our agreement and fill me in on everything."

Kat went to Jimmy and explained the situation.

"You need to get at least two people on the record before we can run with it. We don't need any lawsuits."

"I'll interview the students again and see what I can do." Kat went back to NYU but everyone she talked denied that Mary had been on cocaine. Someone had obviously gotten to them. She went back to the Light and explained the situation to Jimmy.

"You have to leave it out, Kat. That comes from up top."

"Damn it, Jimmy. If it were anyone else you'd let me run with it."

"But it's not. If you want to keep your job, omit the cocaine use from your story."

Furious, Kat went back to her desk. Then she received a phone call. It was the same person that had called her and told her who the body was.

"I'll make a written statement that Mary was a cocaine user."

"I need two reliable sources before I can put it in the paper."

"Go to the diner across the street from you and you'll have your sources."

"What's your name?"

"Timmy Monroe."

~***~

Katherine Hope The New York Light

Senator Charles Monroe's daughter identified

as second victim

October 17th

Mary Monroe, age 20, has been positively identified as the second victim of a serial killer who is somehow connected to the man known only as The Chemist. Ms. Monroe was a sophomore at NYU and used an alias, Edna Smith. She had been stalked by an unnamed male and was reportedly afraid for her life. Timmy Monroe, the victim's younger brother, and Seth Richards, her boyfriend of two years, went on the record stating that Ms. Monroe was a heavy cocaine user. The police department is refusing to cooperate so they will not comment as to whether or not this was a contributing factor in her death. They are listing the cause of death as unknown.

CHAPTER SIX

TIT FOR TAT

Kat called Dante.

I know you're probably angry with me but what can you tell me about Det. Stokes?"

"Why are you asking?"

"Are you familiar with the fire that occurred on October third that killed a family of five at Beacon Heights?"

"Yes."

"I talked to the Arson Investigator and he said Detective Stokes is supposed to be working the case but doesn't seem to be doing anything."

"Maybe he's busy. Not everyone will jump at your beck and call."

"Sorry I bothered you."

The rest of the day was a usual day at work. She received a tip about money laundering through a fake charity. She started digging into it and found some information about the charity. It was supposed to be about helping firefighters. It felt good to write about something other than murder. But she didn't think she'd ever be able to get the images of those poor women out of her mind.

The day went by and still no phone call. Kat felt nothing but relief. She hoped The Chemist would never call her again. The next day was the same and Kat didn't hear from Dante, so she knew there were no new bodies. A week went by. Then two. Kat had enough to write about the money laundering case. She missed Dante and the rapport they had developed but she tried not to think about it. She didn't know if she could ever be involved with anyone again. Jimmy invited her over for dinner, and he and Marge did everything they could to make her feel at home. Maybe because she had come so close to death, she finally admitted to herself that she wanted to be the daughter they wanted her to be. She relaxed in the warm, loving environment and thoroughly enjoyed herself. There had been no repercussions from the Senator. Kat put everything out of her mind and felt happy for the first time since he'd called her.

Then the phone rang.

"Are you aware that Angel (Loco) Rodriguez leader of the gang Los Muertas was gunned down by Jake "Iceman" Turner of the Razors?" It was a young man, with a thick Hispanic accent.

"No, I wasn't. Do you have any proof?"

"Yeah, but I ain't fixing to get killed over it. You know what this means doncha?"

"Gang war."

"Yeah."

"Will you give me your name if I promise to keep it off the record?"

"Hell no."

Kat went to see Jimmy and filled him in on the details.

"Kat this isn't your kind of story. What happened to the money laundering story you were working on?"

"Jimmy. Please understand. I was there, right in the middle of it when Mary Monroe's body was found. I want to write this story."

"Are we going to have to go through this again? What's going on with you? I don't understand this sudden need you have for writing dangerous stories."

"Jimmy, this will be my last one. I promise. Now can you please help me by telling me what I need to do?"

Jimmy sighed out of frustration. Then he told her, "Find out which

Gang Unit is handling the call and see if you can get an interview. But under no circumstances are you to try to interview any gang members unless an arrest is made. Are we clear?"

"Yes."

Kat looked up the information and called The Harlem Gang Division and asked to speak to the lead investigator, Detective White. He made it clear that he didn't want to discuss the case.

"Detective I received a tip and it's enough to write a story," Kat said, hoping he'd take the bait. "It's in your best interest to give me the facts or I will go with what I have."

"We're trying to stop an all-out gang war."

"From what I was told it's too late for that."

"Can you tell your story but leave out the names?"

"I'm afraid not."

"It hasn't been confirmed as to who actually killed Angel Rodriguez. He was shot nine times by someone believed to be driving a black SUV. That's all I know."

"Are there any neutral parties that will try to get involved in stopping the escalation of violence?"

"That I can't answer."

"Thank you, Detective."

After making several more phone calls Kat had enough.

~***~

Katherine Hope The New York Light

Angel "Loco" Rodriguez leader of the gang Los Muertos was gunned down yesterday

October 28th

The Razors have made it known that they intend to take over the streets of New York and are one step closer after the shooting death of the gang leader of Las Muertos. Detective White of the Winchester Gang Division expressed concern that this will start an all-out gang war. There has been a lot of tension between the two gangs since The Razors took over the territory of The Dragons. Thirteen people were killed, including a four-year-old boy, and nine were injured. No arrests were made. The City Council will be convening for a special meeting in search of answers on how to address this growing problem.

~***~

CHAPTER SEVEN

DEAD WOMEN TELL NO LIES

Out of the blue Dante called.

"There's been another murder and we think it's The Chemist."

"Why do you say that?"

"She fits his type. Long blonde hair, green eyes, no obvious signs of a trauma which means it could be poison. She's older than the other two, could be 31 or 32. But we might have caught a break. We found a strand of light brown hair next to the body. The lab is making it their number one priority. If we get lucky, he's in the database."

"I don't know Dante. It's not like him to make a mistake. Besides, why didn't he call me like he did before?"

"I don't have an answer for you. But everyone makes a mistake sooner or later. Can you hold off on writing the story? If it is The Chemist, we don't want to spook him."

"Yes, since the tip came from you."

"Thanks, Kat."

"I want to be able to sit in on the interrogation and interview him afterwards."

"I'll have to check with my captain."

"You do that." Kat couldn't help but think that this story could make her career. Then she remembered Susan Blake's face. *The hell with my career. I want to write this story for them.*

She looked up from what she was writing and saw Jimmy, motioning to her to come in his office.

"What's the latest news from the detective?"

Kat didn't ask how he knew Dante had called.

"I asked him to keep me updated on their progress. They think they may have a break in the case, but they won't know for a couple of days."

"Did the detective tell you what it is?"

"No, he didn't."

"Well, I just hope they catch him so this nightmare will be over. I don't want to have to worry about you all the time."

Kat laughed, "You'll do that anyway and you know it," she said affectionately. It felt so good to be part of something and to know it would last.

"You're right," he said as he returned her smile. Then he got serious.

"I know you're going to cover this case no matter what I say. So, I'm just going to tell you what I say to all my other reporters. Make this paper proud."

"You know I will. But Dante, I mean Detective Russo, asked me not to run the story yet. In exchange, I told him I wanted to be there for his questioning and I want an exclusive interview."

"And he agreed?"

"He said he would check with his captain."

"When was that?"

"About thirty minutes ago."

"Well, since he's waiting for you at your desk I guess you'll get your answer."

Kat turned and saw Dante staring at her. She was surprised

to see him and it made her uncomfortable so she looked away and turned her attention back to Jimmy. "I better see what he has to say."

"Get it in writing. But don't sit on it too long. We don't want any of our competitors to print the story before us. Press him for more information. Remember, they still need you because you're the only one that's ever talked to him. You might be able to help identify him by his voice."

"I'll see what I can do."

"Kat, you're my finest investigative reporter. Don't let me down." The way he said it, she knew he had faith in her. But journalism was a cutthroat business, with everyone racing to get the story first. She couldn't afford to forget that. No matter what.

"Thank you, sir. And I won't let you down." She hurried back to her desk.

"Well?" she asked Dante.

"He agreed. What did your boss have to say?"

"Jimmy wants it in writing. He also expects me to press you to get more information so we can go with a story if it takes too long for you to get a definitive answer."

"What did you tell him?"

"That I'd do my best. I'm going to have to run something soon."

"And I'm trying to catch a killer. I promise I'll let you know as soon as we have something."

"Don't forget, I need it in writing that I'll get to sit in on the interview and that I'll still get an exclusive."

"I won't. Can I fax it to you?"

Kat hesitated. "That should work," she finally said.

After he left she started gathering all her notes together on The Chemist and started outlining what she knew.

The phone rang and it was Dante. "We got a match on the DNA. We're going to pick him up right now. Do you still want to be there for the interview?" asked Dante.

"Of course. Will you be taking him to the 13th Precinct?" Kat was nervous but determined. She wanted that bastard to go to prison for the rest of his life.

"I'll tell the Sergeant at the front desk to bring you to the interrogation room. But you can't do your interview until we know for sure it's him."

"What's the son-of-a-bitch's name?"

"John Pinkton."

"I'll be right there."

Kat took a cab to the police station and as promised she was taken back to the interrogation room.

Surprisingly Dante was outside with his partner. "What's going on?"

"The Crime Scene Unit is still processing his house. We want to let him stew at the same time we want to give them time to gather more evidence."

"Were you ever able to identify the body?"

"No luck. She's not in the system anywhere."

Just then Dante's phone rang. He got out his pen and wrote something down. Then he thanked whomever he was talking to and hung up.

"They found a drug in his bathroom. It's succinylcholine and I was told that anesthesiologists use it after putting a patient under because it causes paralysis and ensures the person being operated on doesn't move during surgery. But without the sedative, the victim can feel everything as their body shuts down. I also learned it's a very painful death. And get this—it can't be detected in the bloodstream. They're bringing it now."

Thirty minutes later a detective brought the bottle in safely inside an evidence bag.

"We found his fingerprints on it along with syringes. I talked to Murph and he told me the drug was difficult to get except through a medical facility. Guess where he works?" asked the investigator from CSU.

"Tell me," said Dante impatiently.

"Stephenson Memorial Hospital."

"I think we've got enough," said Dante's partner, Detective Finley.

"Let me talk to him first," Dante responded. Then he hesitated and checked Pinkton's file. He nodded his head, obviously satisfied by what he read. Dante turned to Kat, "See if you can identify his voice but don't worry if you can't. People sound different over the phone."

Dante went into the interrogation room. There was a metal table with a chair on each side. Pinkton was handcuffed to the table. Dante walked to the table.

"Let's get these off of you, shall we?" Dante said as he removed the handcuffs. "I want you to be comfortable." Dante smiled at him and Kat was amazed by his seemingly friendliness.

How does he do it?

Dante sat across from John Pinkton,

"Good afternoon, John. Is it okay for me to call you that?"

Pinkton nodded his head.

"John, I'm Detective Russo. Is there anything I can get you? I'm afraid I can't recommend the coffee, but we do have a soda machine and bottled water."

John Pinkton didn't say a word, he sat there looking nervous.

"It's alright. I know you've been waiting a while and must be thirsty."

"Do you have Diet Coke?" he asked uncertainly. Kat listened intently to the man's voice. There had never been anything uncertain in the Chemists voice, but he had thought himself safe when he called her, hiding behind his anonymity.

"I believe we do. I'll be right back." Dante exited the room and then went to where Kat was standing behind the one-way glass. “Does it sound like him?”

She hesitated. Her head felt like it was spinning because she knew how much rested on her answer. “I don’t know. I think if I heard him talk some more then...” Her voice trailed off, she was filled with uncertainty.

“It’s alright Kat. Hopefully, I can keep him talking for a while. But regardless, hearing someone speak over the phone can sound different in person. Don’t worry,” Dante said, giving her a smile she knew was meant to be assuring. *If only it worked on me like it worked on Mrs. Watson.*

Dante returned a few moments later with a Diet Coke and a plastic cup full of ice. His partner opened the door for him. Dante entered the room and with a friendly smile set them in front of Pinkton.

“I forgot to ask if you wanted ice, so I brought some just in case.”

Pinkton hesitated. “Do you need some help?” Dante asked. Kat hadn’t noticed it before but Pinkton’s hands were trembling. He nodded his head yes. Dante patiently opened the can and poured some of the beverage in the cup.

“There you go. Take your time.”

Pinkton took a drink and then put the cup down, looking at Dante warily.

“I’m not talking,” Pinkton said, apparently gaining some courage.

“That’s fine. I’ll do the talking and you can just listen. Is that okay, John?”
Dante gave him the same disarming smile. Pinkton relaxed noticeably.

After removing it from his jacket pocket, Dante set the bottle of succinylcholine on the table.

“We found this bottle in your bathroom, along with syringes. We also found one of your hairs at the last crime scene and it was a match for your DNA. It doesn’t look good, John. But maybe you could help me understand because I really want to understand. It's the only way I can help you."

"Why would you do that?"

"Because I'm sure you had a reason. Was it because they were drug users?"

Pinkton shook his head, indicating no.

"They have you directly linked to one murder, it's only a matter of time before they can prove you were responsible for the other two. I need your help."

Silence.

Dante changed tactics. "What was her name?"

"Whose name?"

"The last victim. Surely you don't want her to be buried as a Jane Doe," Dante said softly. "Don't you think her family would like to give her a proper burial? Tell me, John, so I can give them a call."

"Annabel—"

"Annabelle who, John? Come on, you can say it."

"No, you're not going to trick me. I don't want to talk to you anymore," he said, obviously agitated.

"I understand. You must be tired, so I'll come back later." He removed the bottle and quietly left the room.

"It would have been nice to get a confession but at least he didn't lawyer up. Now we have to talk to Murphy," said Dante. He turned to Kat. "You coming?"

They took the trip down to the morgue.

"This place still gives me the chills."

"You get used to it," Dante told her again.

"Hey Murph, what do you know about this drug?" Dante asked as he handed the bottle over to Murphy.

"Well as I told your Crime Scene Guys, SUX as it's known doesn't leave any traces in the bloodstream."

"So, you're telling us there's no way to prove this guy killed Jane Doe using SUX?" asked Kat.

"Pretty much. In some cases, metabolites of SUX can be detected but it's usually a very minor, almost imperceptible, amount. It's easy to miss but this woman was also a cocaine user and that would more than likely make it impossible. But, SUX wouldn't have caused the distortion in her facial features. I'll keep running tests but it could take a while since I don't know what to look for."

"How long is a while?"

Murphy shrugged.

Kat turned to Dante. "So that's it?" she asked.

"No, I'll just have to work harder at getting a confession," Dante said with great determination. "Let's get back to the precinct."

Before they left, Kat looked at the sign in the lobby once again. The dead weren't being much help now.

CHAPTER EIGHT

LIAR, LIAR

On the way back to the precinct, Kat could only think about the fact that the killer might go free.

"I'll nail this guy somehow, Kat." But, to Kat, his words sounded hollow.

As soon as they arrived Dante went looking for his partner. "He say anything?"

"Nobody has been in there."

"Alright, call the hospital where he works and find out what other medications he could have access to that would cause extreme pain when injected and then have them do an inventory. Then go there and make sure they do it asap. We can't take a chance that this guy walks before we have enough evidence."

"Sure thing, Dante."

I'm going to talk to him again." Dante walked by into the interrogation room as Kat watched. "How are you, John?"

"I'm doing okay," Pinkton mumbled.

"We've got the hospital staff doing an inventory of the medications you had access to. It won't be long now. If you want me to help you this is your last chance. Will you talk to me?"

Pinkton looked around nervously. "What exactly can you do

for me?"

"You killed three women, you're definitely going away for life. My bet is you wind up at Southport. It's a supermax and has the reputation as the toughest correctional institute in New York. Or you confess and you get sent to a nicer facility. Some place you could live out the rest of your years comfortably. How about it, John?"

"Can I get that in writing? You know like a guarantee or something?"

"Of course. You agree to confess and we'll take it straight to the District Attorney."

Pinkton looked scared. Finally, he nodded his head.

"John, you have to tell me."

"Okay, I'll give you a confession. But this better not be a trick." He looked at the two-way glass window. "You hear me out there? Better not be a damn trick."

"It's not a trick, I promise you, John. You know you can trust me. I'm the only one that's been looking out for you."

"Alright, just tell me what to say."

"Just tell us about what happened. What was the name of your last victim?"

"Anabelle Pinkton. She was my wife," he said gruffly. "I had to kill that bitch. She was always getting on my nerves, ya know?"

Dante was with him for an hour while he continued to talk about what he had done. But Kat noticed he only talked about the details that had been in the paper. When Dante came out, he had a look of satisfaction. "We got him. It's over now."

But Kat didn't respond, she kept staring at the window as if she looked at it hard enough, she would find the answers she was looking for.

"What's the matter? I thought you'd be happy that it's finally over."

"I don't know, Dante. I'm not convinced it's him."

"Come on, Kat. What more proof do you need? Look at the evidence."

"I'm not saying he didn't kill his wife, I'm just not sure about the other victims."

"His story checked out. Murphy managed to isolate some of the metabolites of succinylcholine, one of which was succinic acid. The hospital completed their inventory of the type of drug we were looking for and said that some rocuronium had been taken. It's used by anesthesiologists also, and it causes severe pain upon injection. Murphy figures Pinkton gave them an injection of rocuronium, and while they were still in pain, shot them up with a lethal dose of SUX. For God sake, what more do you need? Now, go write your story."

Kat smiled at him but looked reluctant. "Fine then. I guess that's what I'll do."

~***~

By Katherine Hope The New York Light

The serial killer responsible for the deaths of three women was found to be The Chemist

October 31st

John Pinkton, 32, was arrested today after the Crime Scene Unit found DNA where his latest victim was discovered. The victim, identified by Pinkton as his wife, Annabelle matched the previous victims' profile. He confessed to the crimes after the one of the substances used to kill his victims as located at his house, and the other substance, was found missing at Stephenson Memorial where he worked. The reign of terror that Mr. Pinkton—a.k.a. The Chemist had over New York is now over.

~***~

Kat sat quietly at her desk, trying to let it all sink in. She was smiling when the phone rang.

CHAPTER NINE

THE JURY IS STILL OUT

Kat knew it was him before she answered the phone. She felt numb when she picked up the receiver but she couldn't bring herself to say a word. So, she sat silently holding the phone until the terrible sound of his voice broke the silence.

"Hello dear. You made a

big mistake."

How could she not have known it wasn't Pinkton? That voice...

"I'm so sorry. I'll print a retraction. It'll be out tomorrow morning." But she knew that wouldn't be good enough for him. She was terrified.

"You really think that will make up for the way you smeared my name? No, someone close to you is going to pay for your sins. Goodbye, Kat."

The way he said it sounded so permanent that for a moment she thought he would come after her. But no, it was worse. He was going to kill someone close to her. The horror of it struck her as she realized the only people it could be were Dante, Jimmy and Marge.

"Oh, dear God."

Kat called Dante and told him what happened and about what she feared.

"I'm so sorry, Kat. We were so sure we had him. Damn it. Does Marge work?"

"No, she doesn't. She should be at home."

"I'll send a patrol car over to stay with her until we can make better arrangements. What about Jimmy? Is he still at the paper?"

Kat had already checked on Jimmy the moment after The Chemist hung up. She felt terror worse than anything she experienced before, and she didn't think that was possible. She felt helpless, a feeling she despised because she had sworn to herself that she would never be in that position again.

"He's in his office."

"Do you think you can talk to him and let him know what's going on?"

"Yes," she answered shakily.

"Keep an eye on him until I get there."

After Kat composed herself the best she could, she went to Jimmy's office, closed the door and filled him in. She didn't omit anything. He had the right to know.

"I'm so sorry I made you and Marge targets."

"No, you didn't. We did that when we decided to make you an unofficial member of the family. If we all survive this, we'll have to see about making it permanent. If that's alright with you," he said quietly.

"Thank you, Jimmy, you have no idea what that means to me," Kat said wistfully. Then she became all business. "Right now, I want to focus on how to keep everyone alive."

"How soon can you print a retraction?"

"I'll write it now but it won't come out until tomorrow morning's edition."

"I know. There's nothing to do but write the retraction and

then let the police do their jobs."

"I'm going to write it now. Kate raced back to her desk, and stared at her computer monitor, thinking how to best approach the story. Then, she started writing. It took her only ten minutes. Kat sent it to Jimmy for his approval, which she received no more than a minute later. She then sent it on to Pre-Press and followed up with a call to the supervisor, a man she knew well. He was very thorough and good at his job, but Kat wasn't taking any chances.

"Hi, Peter. The retraction I sent you is extremely important and it has to be the frontpage headline in the morning, afternoon, and evening editions. I can't stress enough how crucial it is. Can you make sure that happens?"

"Of course. I won't let you down," he said in a tone that Kat found reassuring. She could tell he was all business. All Kat could do now was wait, but she didn't know how she could stand to do it alone. She hesitated when she saw Dante in Jimmy's office, but Jimmy had seen her and motioned for her to join them.

"I don't suppose you have anything to say for yourself since all this is your fault," Kat said ferociously. She felt so strongly about Jimmy and Marge, she didn't realize how fiercely she sounded. "If anything happens I will never forgive you. I told you about my doubts and you ignored me." The thought of striking Dante crossed her mind, and she couldn't let it go. Without realizing it, she started to raise her hand. The sound of Jimmy's voice stopped her.

"Kat, you're being unfair. The evidence was there."

"For the third murder, I agree. But there was no concrete evidence connecting him to the first two victims."

Jimmy wasn't through. "John Pinkton sighed a confession and he took credit for their deaths."

"Of course he did. After Detective Russo told Pinkton he could live out his life at Ryker's Island, the best of the state penitentiaries, instead of going to the Supermax, where his life would have been hell. Under those terms who wouldn't confess?" Kat said, her voice was filled with contempt.

"Kat, I think it would be best if you went home and got some rest. Detective Russo has assigned someone to accompany you at all times." Jimmy looked at her sternly.

"I know you, Kat, listen to the man," Jimmy said........

"Yes, sir."

Officer Miller was waiting for her in the lobby. Just as she had promised, she followed his instructions. Even as tired as she was, she couldn't sleep. In the morning she just wanted to get to the paper but Officer Miller insisted on checking everything. She grew weary and thought about dumping him, but then remembered her promise to Jimmy.

First thing she did was check the paper. There it was. She read it again.

In big bold letters the headline read:

~***~

By Katherine Hope The New York Light

John Pinkton is not the man known as the Chemist

November 1st

The Chemist has claimed responsibility for the first two deaths in a murder spree that has left the police baffled, but denies any connection to the third woman, who turned out to be John Pinkton's wife. The Chemist was angered by the article that was in yesterday's paper, when Pinkton took responsibility for all the deaths and even signed a confession. The evidence clearly showed he had murdered his wife, whom he claimed, "Was always getting on his nerves."

The man only known as the Chemist has promised retaliation because of the article in yesterday's paper. Although he has proved to be elusive, he is believed to be a Caucasian male, in his early to mid-thirties, approximately 5'11" and has short light brown hair. He has a background in science with access to poisonous drugs. The police have set-up a tip line. If you have any information call (212)555-1867. This man is extremely dangerous so always use caution and the police are advising women not to go anywhere unless they are accompanied by another adult. The New York City police department have made the capture of this cold-blooded killer their number one priority.

Kat's phone rang. Hello dear."

"I saw your article. Very clever. Now I'll give you the location of the next body. There's a service elevator at the back of your building. It's jammed shut because I wanted you to be there when they find him."

The Chemist hung up and then Kat had the most terrifying thought. Jimmy wasn't in his office. She went to the center of the newsroom and stood on Rick's desk. "Has anybody seen Jimmy?" she yelled as loud as she could.

"I saw him leave earlier, he seemed to be in a hurry," replied Paul. He was the reporter who wrote obits.

"What time was that?"

"About ten."

"Oh my God, this is my fault." She immediately called Dante and told him about the call and her suspicion.

"I'll be there in fifteen minutes. Whatever you do don't touch anything and keep everyone away."

Kat reached the service elevator in no time. It took all her willpower not to ask one of the workers inside the dock to try to pry the elevator doors open. She found herself praying it wasn't Jimmy. What seemed like hours later she heard the sound of a siren and Dante pulled up and quickly went to get a crowbar from the trunk of his unmarked car. His partner Det. Finley was with him. All she wanted to do was get the elevator doors open.

Dante climbed up on the loading dock and Kat had an irrational thought and hoped he didn't get his suit dirty. She noticed his partner used the stairs and she instantly disliked him. Then Dante was by her side and he took his crowbar but couldn't get the end in between the two doors. He asked his partner to check with the gathering crowd to see if he could get a sledgehammer. Kat saw him disappear inside with one of the workers. Just then two patrol cars showed up. The police officers got out and went to the dock and two of them ensured the gathering crowd did not get too close while the other two approached to see if they could help. Dante filled them in on what was going on and told them to start asking everyone if they had seen anything suspicious. He also told them to get everyone's name and to take pictures of the crowd.

So far Kat hadn't said a word. She was frozen with fear. Detective Russo looked at her and she could tell he was talking to her but couldn't make out the words. Next thing she knew he was shaking her and this time she could hear him although it seemed surreal.

"Kat snap out of it. Come on, Kat. You're tough, remember? You can deal with this."

She looked at him with tears in her eyes. "You don't understand, this is all my fault."

"No, it isn't. I screwed up. Now I want you to go with policeman Smith here and give him your statement," Dante said while pointing to the taller of the two.

"No, I can't. I have to see if it is Jimmy."

"The best thing you can do is help us catch this sadistic son-of-a-bitch and you can do that by giving your statement."

He looked at the police officer. "Will you take Ms. Hope and get her statement?"

The police Officer gently touched her arm. "Come with me, Ms."

Feeling like she was in a trance she followed him and started telling him what happened. Then she noticed Dante's partner return with a sledgehammer. Kat turned to watch. She saw Dante holding the crowbar as he placed it in what little room there was where the doors met and his partner started hitting the end of it. They didn't make any progress. However The Chemist sealed the doors, it was obvious they needed help. Kat overheard a police officer tell Dante how odd it was because service elevators are usually designed to open easily.

Kat heard Dante tell his partner to call the fire department so they could bring the jaws of life. A fire truck arrived not ten minutes later bringing the tool with them.

She listened to one of the firefighters tell Dante, "Whoever did this was smart. We should be able to use our fire service key to open the doors but someone epoxied the keyhole mechanism."

"He was smart," reverberated through Kat's head until she thought it would explode. The Chemist was always one step ahead of them. She watched the Firefighters struggle until they were able to get the doors open. Terrified at what she would see, Kat walked towards the open elevator. Dante saw her and walked towards her and stopped her.

"You don't want to see."

"Yes, I do. Now let me get by."

"Kat."

"Move out of my way," Kat said angrily.

Dante moved but stayed close by her side.

When she reached the opening, she looked inside and cried out, "No!"

It was Jimmy, only she could barely recognize him. He had been placed on a chair and fastened to it using a piece of rope so his face was easily seen. It was contorted in agony and he had vomited so that his chin and the front of his shirt were covered in it. She started to enter the elevator but Dante stopped her.

"The Crime Scene Unit has to process the area and we can't take the risk of contaminating it. I'm sorry you can't go near his body until the Coroner has a chance to examine him at the morgue."

“Don’t refer to him like he’s nobody. His name is Jimmy Brooks, and he’s one of the best editors that ever lived.” She realized she’d been speaking about him in the present tense even though she was looking at his lifeless body. Somehow that made the whole situation worse so she had to fight back the tears. Then, Kat collected herself and decided how to ensure Jimmy got the respect he deserved. One of the police officers approached Dante.

“Everyone swears they didn’t see anyone near the elevator.”

“Take all their statements and see if there was anyone working that might have left,” Dante instructed him.

Kat turned to leave.

“Where are you going?”

“To get my notepad and pens. Someone has to write this story and it might as well be me.”

Dante didn’t try and stop her. If he had, Kat was so determined she probably would have struck him. When she arrived at the News Room everyone was staring at her.

“Where’s Jimmy?” she heard someone say but she didn’t look to see who.

‘He’s dead,” she replied, in a monotone. Kat heard overlapping voices but she ignored them all and got what she needed. She wanted to be prepared. Then, she headed back down the stairs so she could get to the service elevator. She saw the Crime Scene Unit had arrived and then a woman exited the elevator. Kat walked up to Dante.

“Who is she and what is she doing?”

“Kat you can’t be here. You need to go behind the yellow tape and let us do our jobs.”

“Like hell I will.”

“Kat you have no choice.” He turned to a uniformed police officer standing nearby. “Officer, escort Ms. Hope from the crime scene.”

“You bastard,” she said to Dante.

The officer politely said, "Please come with me, Ms."

"Fine," she retorted. She went and joined the ever-growing number of bystanders. Then, she started taking pictures of everyone who entered the elevator using her cell phone. Frustrated, she tried to hear as much as she could but as far away as she was, she couldn't hear but bits and pieces of the conversations. Eventually, she saw Jimmy being removed in a body bag. It took everything she had to hold back the tears. Then she saw Dante heading towards her.

"Let's go somewhere we can talk."

Kat led him to the side of the building where there was no one else.

"We had a deal."

"Which I intend to honor. It looks like he was also poisoned although we won't know more until the autopsy is performed."

"I already knew that," she said angrily. "Now tell me something I don't know."

"I can only tell you that CSU hasn't found anything that they think will be helpful in identifying the killer but I have to ask that you don't print that."

"Why not? The public needs to know how inept our police are."

"That's not fair, Kat."

"It's Ms. Hope to you, Det. Russo."

Dante sighed. "I'm not the enemy here."

"Well, you're certainly not a friend. Do you have any official statement you'd like to make?"

"The New York City Police Department will use all its resources to stop the killer."

Kat scoffed. "Can I talk to the woman that is in charge of the Crime Scene Unit? What's her name?"

"Rebecca Peterson. I'll see if she'll talk to you. Wait here." Dante disappeared around the corner. He returned 15 minutes later with Rebecca. She was all business.

"Detective Russo tells me that you're the reporter the man who calls himself The Chemist calls."

"Yes, I am."

"Would you allow us to tap your phone so we can try to trace his calls?"

"Absolutely not. My sources expect strict confidentiality. I can't exactly have that with the police listening. That's what Jimmy would want me to do," she added, as it dawned on her that even though her friend and mentor was dead, remembering the lessons he taught her was something even his killer couldn't take away from her.

"I could always get a court order."

Kat laughed, but it showed nothing but disdain. "Good luck with that. I'm going to call our attorney as soon as I get back to my desk. Now I have questions for you."

"I'll answer what I can."

"Were you able to get any forensic evidence that might give you any leads?"

"The elevator had been thoroughly cleaned. From what we could tell it was wiped down with ammonia. No prints anywhere. The only hair we found looked like it belonged to Mr. Brooks. Whoever this guy is, he proved once again that he knows what he's doing. But that's something we don't want in the paper. In fact, I'd like you to print that we have a lead."

"No, he'll know I'm lying and kill someone else I love. And I want to catch the son-of-a-bitch."

"We all do, Ms. Hope. But the worst thing you can do is let it be personal."

"It is personal. He didn't just kill my boss, he killed a dear friend. And it's my fault." Her body started to tremble and she felt weak in the knees.

"Detective Russo told me what happened. But you shouldn't

blame yourself. There's no way you could have known. Now, if you'll excuse me I have work to do."

"So do I. I have a story to write."

"Kat, are you going to be okay?"

"I told you it's Ms. Hope and that's none of your concern. One other thing."

"Yes?"

"I'm going with you to inform his wife."

"Dante sighed. "Kat that's—"

"That really wasn't a question."

With that, she left.

CHAPTER TEN

BID ADIEU

Kat kept busy while she waited for Dante but couldn't get the image of Jimmy out of her head. She found Cindy sitting at her desk sobbing hysterically. It took several minutes before she calmed down enough to answer questions.

"I know this is difficult but I need to understand what happened," Kat said soothingly. She managed to get Cindy to look her in the eyes so she could try and keep her focused.

"Do you know where Jimmy was going and why?"

Cindy let out a small sob. "He just said he was going to meet a source about a story."

"That's unusual. Did he say why he didn't hand it off to a reporter?"

"I thought it was strange too but I just thought he had a good reason."

"Is there anything else you can tell me?"

"I noticed he seemed nervous."

"Did you ask him why?"

"Yes. He just said it was a big story." Then she started sobbing again.

Kat patted her on the back and thanked her.

Next, she went to interview Paul.

"You said you saw Jimmy leaving around ten. Did he seem to be acting any differently than usual?"

"Well, I said good morning to him and he didn't acknowledge me. Jimmy is, I mean was, never too busy to take a minute for his employees." His voice had started quivering and she could tell he was close to tears. Kat felt bad pressing him.

"You said he left around 10. Do you know what the exact time was?"

"9:52. I remember since I had just checked because I had to call about an obit at 10." He paused for a minute, as something dawned on him and his voice grew even sadder.

"I guess I'll be writing his obit."

"Just write it so you can tell your readers what a great man he was. That's something you can do for Jimmy."

Paul nodded, and his mouth formed a small smile but his eyes looked sad.

"It'll be the best obit I've ever written. Thanks, Kat." Then he looked at her as something appeared to dawn on him. "How are you holding up? I know how close you and Jimmy were."

"Honestly, I feel numb. I'm just trying to concentrate on my story."

"If you need someone to talk to . . ."

"Thanks, Paul. I appreciate it. If you think of anything let me know."

Kat interviewed more of the reporters but none of them had anything to add. She returned to her desk and started writing the article, leaving space for the questions she needed to ask Dante.

"You ready?" She looked up to see Dante.

"Yes, I just need to grab my things." She put her notepad and pens in her bag and then stood up. "I'm ready." Without a word, they rode the elevator down to the first floor and Kat followed him to where he had parked his Impala.

"I need to ask you some questions for my article."

"Ask whatever you need to."

"When Jimmy left the building where was his police protection?" She managed to keep the bitterness out of her voice.

"He was supposed to notify the officer and didn't. Apparently, he slipped out."

"Do you know what exit he used?"

"The employee exit on the west side of the building."

"That leads to the parking lot. Were they able to see where he went from there?"

"No, he evaded the cameras."

"Damn."

They rode the rest of the way in silence. When they arrived, the patrol car was still out front. Kat got out first and headed for the door but Dante caught up to her quickly. She rang the doorbell and it didn't take long for Marge to respond. She was ten years younger than Jimmy but appeared younger. She always took care of herself and was nicely dressed regardless of whether she planned to go anywhere or not. Today was no exception.

"Hi Kat. What a pleasant surprise," she said cheerfully. Then she looked at Dante.

"You must be Det. Russo. I'm Marge," she said as she held out her hand and shook his.

Kat had rehearsed everything she planned to say but Marge's demeanor was too much. She seemed so happy. How could she destroy that?

Marge saw the look on Kat's face and asked, "What's wrong?"

Kat opened her mouth to speak but nothing came out.

Dante took over. "Do you mind if we come in?"

"No. Please do," Marge said, her voice filled with concern.

After they entered Marge gestured towards the couch and said, "Have a seat. Is there anything I can get you?"

"No, thanks," Dante responded. Kat still couldn't bear to say a word.

"I'm afraid I have some bad news." His voice, although he remained professional, showed his sympathy.

"It's about Jimmy, isn't it? Something bad happened."

"I'm afraid so. He was killed this morning."

"Oh, God. Not my Jimmy!" She was close to tears. "Was it The Chemist?" she asked, her voice was filled with fear.

"Yes, ma'am. I'm afraid so."

"Oh, no. He suffered a lot, didn't he?" Kat could hear the horror in her voice.

"It appears so."

"How soon can I see him?"

"I don't think that's a good idea. We can get someone else to ID him."

"No. And that's not what I asked."

"I'll put in a call to the medical examiner," Dante said reluctantly.

As Dante made his call, Marge turned to Kat. "How are you holding up?"

Kat struggled to find the words to say. "Honestly I don't think it's sunk in yet."

"If you need someone to talk to, please, come see me." Kat thought she was the most selfless person she knew.

"Oh, Marge." Kat was overwhelmed by emotion.

Then Dante interrupted. "I talked to the Medical Examiner. He said we can come in now."

"Let me grab a sweater." She returned a few minutes later. "Let's go."

When they walk outside, Dante said, "Go ahead and get in. I need to speak to the officer."

Marge got in the back seat while Kat took her place upfront. She looked in the rearview mirror and saw the squad car leave. Dante returned to the driver's side and got in.

"Do you want me to drop you off at the paper, Kat?"

"No, I'm going." Kat was resolved to stay with Marge even though she didn't know if she could bear the sight again.

When they arrived, Dante parked and they entered the morgue. Murph was waiting for them. He looked at Marge. "Are you ready?"

"Yes." Marge said. Somehow, she had managed to seem composed.

"Okay."

Murph went to the drawers and opened one pulling out the tray. There was Jimmy. Kat struggled to keep herself from gasping. Outwardly, Marge remained calm, but Kat knew her well enough to know that it was a facade.

Murph asked, "Can you state his name for the records?" Then added, "And your relationship to the deceased."

"His name is James Edward Burke. I'm his wife. Margaret Elizabeth Burke. When will you release his body? I need to make arrangements."

"I need to wait until the police tell me I can release him. I'll call you as soon as I know something. You have my sincere condolences."

"Thank you."

"I'll take you home," Dante told her.

"Thank you, Detective."

"I'll take a cab," Kat said.

"You sure?"

"Positive."

"Alright, call me if I can help in any way."

They left and Kat called a cab. She spent the ride there thinking about what she would write.

~***~

By Katherine Hope The New York Light

Editor James Burke brutally murdered by The Chemist for printing the false confession of John Pinkton

November 2nd

In retaliation for printing the incorrect identification of John Pinkton as The Chemist the real Chemist brutally murdered edi-tor James "Jimmy" Burke. It appears that the cause of death was poison, the same method used to kill the other victims but an au-topsy must be performed to confirm that. Jimmy will be greatly missed and was beloved by all.

CHAPTER ELEVEN

YOU DID WHAT?

The phone rang.

It was Dante. "The alarm went off on the camera in the hall across from your apartment door. It's him."

"Let's go."

"No, it's too dangerous. What's the code?"

"4521."

"I'll call you when it's all clear. You have a

computer at home, don't you?"

"I'll bring my laptop."

Kat couldn't wait so she called for a cab. It was 45 minutes before he called again.

"Do you want me to pick you up or would you rather take a cab?"

"I'm in a cab right now and I'm almost there."

When she arrived, Dante had the memory card out and then went inside Kat's apartment and put it in her laptop's sim card slot and reviewed the footage but once again he had his face fairly well covered so she couldn't see much. But something bothered her although she couldn't quite grasp what it was.

"Let's check and see if he left me another note."

There was one. "Let me," Dante said, as he started to reach for the vase.

Kat reached out and stopped him. "No, I'll do it. Then she lifted the vase and read it silently. At first, she wasn't sure what he meant. Then Kat remembered what Rebecca had said.

Kat was livid. "What did it say?" Dante asked.

"I think you'd better go. I have something I need to do."

"Kat if you think I'm going to let you go off and do something stupid—"

"Don't worry. It's nothing like that." She forced a smile.

"Then let me read the note," Dante insisted.

"I promise it's not threatening. I'm leaving as soon as I call a cab."

"At least let me give you a ride."

"I'm sure you have better things to do than act as my chauffeur. Now please go so I can make that phone call." Kat went to her front door and opened it. Reluctantly, Dante left.

After the cab arrived, she got in and looked at the driver's cab permit.

"Reginald, take me to the Olympic Building. There's $100 in it for you if you can get me there in 15 minutes." Without hesitation, he took off and drove like a madman, weaving in and out of traffic, accelerating when he could, only to slam on the brakes in order to swerve into an open lane. They got there in fourteen minutes. Reginald smiled at her as he held out his hand. After paying him she went inside and talked to one of the security guards, Paul, and asked him to follow her. The reporters that were there as she walked into the room looked at her oddly but didn't say a word. Kat went to her desk and picked up the handset of her phone, unscrewed the end that covered the mouthpiece, and there it was. The bug.

"Paul, I need you as my witness. Do you recognize what this is?" she asked as she pointed towards the tiny electronic device.

"No, ma'am."

Kat sighed impatiently. "Someone has bugged my phone. I need your statement testifying to what you saw. In writing." She grabbed a piece of paper and a pen off her desk and handed them to him. While he was writing she took several pictures and then using a tissue carefully removed the device and put it in one of the side compartments in her bag and zipped it closed. After Paul was done writing she also placed that in her bag.

Normally, Kat would have told Jimmy, but he wasn't here. She hadn't allowed herself to really grieve. She knew she should see Marge but then it would be real and she couldn't bear the thought. The next step was to see the supervising editor. Jimmy's boss. He was the kind of man that intimidated most people, but then Kat was not easily intimidated. She called and made an appointment to see him at 2 p.m. It was only 10. She had four hours to kill.

Then she saw someone going into Jimmy's office and sit in his chair. Outraged, she went to see what the hell he was doing. He looked to be in his early thirties and had a cocky air about him.

"What the hell are you doing here? This is Jimmy's office."

"You must be Kat." His voice was smooth and easygoing. But Kat had a feeling that it could change in a minute if something displeased him. "I'm Brad Milton. Your new editor." Kat had been expecting it but was still shocked. Nobody could replace Jimmy. "I've heard a lot of good things about you. I understand you and Jimmy were close and I know I can't replace him. But I know if you give me a chance you'll find I'm a pretty good guy and that I'm very knowledgeable. I've got a lot of experience in journalism." He gave her a warm smile and she felt her anger dissipate.

"There's something else I wanted to talk to you about. This came from up high. They want you to write a tribute about Jimmy. It's going to be on the front page and you can use as much space as you want."

The more he talked the more she wanted to run. It would mean facing the unfathomable and she didn't know if she could survive that. It had taken Kat a while but she finally had come to realize that Jimmy's death wasn't all her fault. Yes, she had turned off the investigative reporter and become a witness and hadn't pushed enough when she had her doubts. But the police had found him guilty and she had wanted to believe so badly she went along with it. She could only hope that Marge would understand.

On the drive to Jimmy's house, she tried to think of what to say. Kat hadn't allowed herself to mourn Jimmy's loss because she couldn't face the thought without crumbling. Something she couldn't afford to do. When she arrived she rang the doorbell, half hoping that Marge wouldn't be there but she knew that was the cowardly way out. Even though she had seen her since Jimmy's death she still didn't know if could face her. She was a reminder of Jimmy and every time she let even a little bit of what had happened she felt lost.

Marge opened the door and when she saw Kat her whole face lit up.

"Kat dear, come in here and give me a hug." But it was too much to bear. She fell into Marge's arms and started sobbing, the deep wretched kind that only came from great loss. She felt safe in Marge's arms. The warm loving woman who she thought of as the mother she never had.

"Okay Kat, compose yourself and come sit on the couch and talk to me. Jimmy wouldn't want to see you like this. You're a strong young woman, and he admired you so much for that."

"Thank you, Marge." They went and sat on the couch, close together. Kat felt herself gain strength from Marge but she felt Marge gained something from her too.

"The paper wants me to write a memorial on Jimmy but I've decided to make it a tribute instead. Do you mind if I asked you some questions?"

"Of course not, dear."

"How did you and Jimmy meet and knowing Jimmy, I assume he didn't ask you to marry him the traditional manner," she smiled when she said it.

Marge started laughing. "You could say that. I was working as a junior reporter in Metro. I covered minor stories since I was so new. I had written a story about a restaurant opening. I'll never forget its name, 'La Cucina Bella.' I was rather proud of myself and had laid it on the editor's desk. The next thing I know Jimmy was standing there. I had never officially been introduced and to be honest I found him intimidating as most people did. He asked me what did I think I was doing turning in such a crappy article? His voice was raised and he had that stern look on his face. I'm sure you know the one." She looked at Kat expectantly.

"I definitely do. I was on the receiving end more than once."

Marge laughed again and really seemed to be enjoying herself.

"Then he sat down with me and patiently showed me how to correct it and explained things with me that nobody had ever taken the time to. I turned the article in and my editor made a point of stopping by and telling me what a great job I had done. He was so pleased I didn't have the heart to tell him Jimmy had helped me. After that, every day Jimmy and I met for lunch in the break room and he helped me with whatever piece I was writing. Then one day he told me he had decided to take me out to dinner. Just like that. So, we went to this nice restaurant. I knew he couldn't afford it and was trying to impress me. I looked over at him and said, 'Jimmy, I don't need all this, I'm already impressed.' After that, he cooked for me at his apartment. He was such a wonderful cook," Marge said, wistfully.

"I remember," said Kat hoping to get her out of the mood, not wanting her to descend into the dark pits of her grief. "So, tell me how he proposed."

That brought a smile to Marge's face. "I don't know if you can call it a proposal dear." She looked at Kat and was practically beaming.

"Jimmy was never very conventional."

Marge laughed. "One night after dinner, Jimmy said, 'I've decided that we're getting married. Hold out your left hand.' Speechless I did what he said and he put on a lovely engagement ring onto my finger. I later found out it had been his grandmothers. A month later we were married." Marge started laughing again and Kat could tell she was lost in the moment. Then there was an awkward silence. "Kat dear, I think you know how much Jimmy loved you. He also worried about you all the time after that dreadful incident." Marge looked at Kat and must have seen Kat's expression because she changed the subject. "I want you to feel like you are always welcome. Just because Jimmy's gone doesn't mean you're not still a part of this family." She paused, then added, "However small it is now." Kat gave Marge a long hug and felt Marge's body tremble but she didn't cry. Kat admired her bravery. Then she pulled away and being the selfless person that she was Marge turned her attention back to Kat.

"I know Jimmy's death must be particularly hard on you. You've never talked much about it but I know your parents died when you were young and you grew up in foster care. I can't begin to imagine how hard that was on you. And then you accepted Jimmy as your father only to have him taken away so soon after. But I hope you'll accept me. Jimmy and I were never blessed with children but if I could have had a daughter I would have wanted her to be just like you." There were tears in her eyes. Kat realized she was also crying.

She reached out and took Marge's hand, "My foster parents saw me as a way of getting money from the government. I used to lie awake at night wishing some nice family would come along and adopt me. It may have taken a lot longer than I expected but I'd be honored to have you as my mother."

"Good. Now that that is settled I wanted to talk to you about Dante."

"There's nothing to talk about."

"Jimmy told me everything so I know you have feelings for

him. In spite of what happened, reach out to him. Don't let him get away or you'll wind up regretting it."

"I will. Thanks, Marge." Kat knew she was right but then looked at her watch. She'd spent more time than she expected. If she wanted to make her 2:00 p.m. appointment she really had to hurry.

CHAPTER TWELVE

SAYING GOODBYE

Kat made it back in time. She knocked Peter Stafford's door and he told her to come in. She took a seat in a chair directly in front of him. "So, what can I do for you, Kat?"

She pulled the tissue with the bug out of her bag along with the signed statement from the security guard "Somebody put a bug in my phone and I have a pretty good idea."

"Is that so? Mind if I see it?" Kat handed him the bug. "I also have a sworn statement from a security guard who saw it in the receiver on my phone."

"Why would anyone want to bug your phone?"

She paused for a moment. She had managed to go most of the day without thinking about him.

"Because Rebecca Peterson, the head of the Crime Scene unit that came when Jimmy was murdered, thought it would help them catch The Chemist. But I told them no. That's what Jimmy would have done," Kat added fiercely.

He simply nodded his head, "Well, leave them with me and I promise you I'll get to the bottom of this." Then he gave a look that meant the conversation was over but she left feeling uneasy. Somehow, Kat knew he wasn't going to do anything about it. He didn't seem surprised at all and couldn't wait to get rid of her. She thought of Marge's words and decided to call Dante from her cell. He seemed surprised to hear from her and from the way their last conversation ended she couldn't blame him.

"I wanted to apologize to you. I know you were only doing your job and following police procedure with Pinkton. I don't blame you for Jimmy's death."

"Well, that makes one of us. You had doubts and I should have listened to them."

"Dante you know as well as I do someone from above would have forced your hand. Now would you quit wallowing in self-pity long enough to help me out?"

"Whatever you need."

"That's what I like to hear."

Dante laughed and Kat thought that he probably hadn't done that in a while.

"Someone bugged my phone at the paper."

"Let's meet somewhere. Do you know where Sally's is on 15th and Washington?"

"No, but I'm sure my cab driver will."

"Okay, see you there."

Kat was fortunate and was able to get a cab right away. She arrived at Sally's twenty minutes later and spotted Dante right away, sitting in a corner booth on the far side of the diner. She smiled when she saw him and thought about the dinner they had. When she arrived at his table he stood up and kissed her on the cheek. Then he got down to business.

"Do you still have the bug?"

"No, one of my bosses insisted I give it but I did take pictures of it.'"

Kat took out her camera and found the photos then handed it to him.

"Yeah, that's definitely one of ours. I wish you'd come to me first but it's a good thing you have pictures."

"And a witness."

"I'm not sure how much good that will do us."

Kat liked the way he said "us". "I'll email the pictures to your phone right now."

"Thanks, Kat. Since we're here you want to grab a bite to eat?"

"Now that you mention it, I haven't had lunch and I'm starving."

After they finished their lunch Kat realized she'd better get back so she could conduct the interviews and get more for Jimmy's Tribute. After she returned to the paper she managed to track down a man she was told was a friend of his when they both started at the paper. His name was Kevin Boone.

"Hi Kevin, I'm Katherine Hope and I'm writing a Tribute for Jimmy. I understand you started out together. Can you tell me about what it was like? I'm especially looking for something would stand out as a memorable moment."

Kevin gave her a mischievous grin. "Jimmy was Jimmy. Everything about the man was memorable. Jimmy and I started writing ads which were a considerable waste of his talent but he never complained and did his best. We used to have lunch together every day in the break room. Until he met Marge. I knew he was in love the first minute he saw her. Something memorable about Jimmy? He wanted to become a reporter but knew he had to get someone's attention.

"One of the priorities of the paper was to catch the Mayor for taking bribes and allowing the mob to run 75% of the construction business in the city. Needless to say, it was very dangerous but that didn't scare Jimmy off. He wrote the story, included his by-line along with a note telling them where they could find him. After verifying the facts, the paper ran the story, giving credit to the police for exposing the truth. The Mayor was forced to resign and Jimmy became a reporter."

"Thanks, that sounds like Jimmy."

"Look, Kat, I know you and Jimmy were close. I'm really sorry about what happened."

"That means a lot. Can you tell me of someone else I could talk to?"

"Sure, Adrian Demopoulas. He's in Florida now near his in-laws. He wasn't too happy about the move but his wife was a real nag and he eventually gave in."

"Do you know where in Florida?"

"Miami."

Kat called Miami information and wrote down his number then called him. She didn't expect him to be there that time of day but he answered on the second ring.

"This is Kat Hope from the New York Light. I'd like to speak to Adrian Demopoulas."

"You got him. I was expecting a call from you. You're doing a tribute to Jimmy."

"I am."

"Well, I know what you want. I worked for Jimmy when he first became a journalist. He was ferocious. He didn't walk away from anything. And he never hesitated to call out our boss, Max Guterre, and he was never wrong. Max hated him and tried to find an excuse to fire Jimmy. Something must have happened because after that he left Jimmy alone. It wasn't long before Max was fired and Jimmy got his job."

Kat had enough material to write the story.

CHAPTER THIRTEEN

STRAIGHT FROM THE HORSE'S MOUTH

The phone rang. It was Dante.

We've had a psychiatrist step forward and he thinks he can help us find The Chemist. He's picked someone for us to look at."

"You going to let me watch the interrogation?"

"Of course. I'm sending a car to pick you up."

"Thanks. I'll be ready."

When Kat arrived at the precinct, she was escorted to the interrogation room Three. Dante was standing next to a distinguished looking man wearing an expensive suit. Dante smiled at her and she was surprised because he rarely smiled. "I'd like to introduce you to Dr. Byron Black. Dr. Black this is Katherine Hope from The New York Light."

"It's a pleasure to meet you, Ms. Hope," he said, and Kat's first impression was that he was very charming.

"Call me Katherine."

"And you can call me Byron, dear."

The fact that he called her dear made her feel uneasy.

"Do you mind if I take notes?"

"That will be fine," said Byron.

Kat took out her notepad and pen.

"What's his name and why did you pick him?"

"His name is Peter Volkner and Detective Russo gave me the case files of persons of interest and he fit the profile."

"What do you know about serial killers?"

"I've been fascinated with them since college. I studied everything I could."

"What insights can you provide?"

"I think we're looking for a man who has suffered under unfortunate circumstances."

"What kind of circumstances?"

"Some kind of severe trauma or a betrayal at an early age. He grew up feeling unloved. He will act to any betrayal so, as I explained to Dante, he needs to show Volkner he's on his side. We conducted interviews with his co-workers who described him as a loner. They also said he was efficient and a great planner. His social behavior, for the most part, is acceptable although he has been known to break the rules. He is probably quite intelligent and cunning. Dante, make sure you have thorough knowledge of the crimes. He won't be intimidated by threats so treat him as if you need his help. Show that you respect him. Don't react emotionally to anything he says. He feels superior and wants to brag about his crime. He obviously wants attention or he wouldn't be calling a reporter about his crimes. One other thing, make sure your badge is in view at all times. Be careful, Detective. He's going to try and outsmart you so make sure you stay in charge while questioning him."

"Thanks, Byron. I'm going to start my interrogation now," said Dante, who then went into the interrogation room. He had Volkner's file, the file on The Chemist, along with a notepad, a pen and a recorder. He sat down across from Volkner and smiled at him in a friendly manner.

"Hello Mr. Volkner, I'm Detective Russo but you can call me Dante." His demeanor was pleasant.

"Dante, why am I here?" he asked suspiciously.

"We're looking into the deaths of several young women and I was hoping you might help me."

"And why should I do that?"

"I just thought a man of your intelligence could help."

"What did they look like?" he asked, looking completely unconcerned.

"Long blonde hair, green eyes, early twenties, approximately five feet seven inches tall, 120 to 130 pounds."

"Not my type," Volkner replied smugly.

"What is your type?"

"Why should I tell you?" he asked guardedly.

"Only because I admire this man's work and I'd like to tell him. And we need your help," Dante whispered.

"I have a genius IQ," he bragged.

"I know. I was so fascinated I knew you had to have a remarkable background. Not many people can have the accomplishments you've had at such a young age. You graduated at only 22 with a doctorate in chemistry and your thesis was about how the most common poisons are used by serial killers and why they wouldn't work with modern day forensics. That sounds quite fascinating and I'd love to read it."

Volkner smiled proudly. "I'm sure that could be arranged."

"You said the blondes weren't your taste. What are?"

"I like pretty brunettes, young ones."

This caused a reaction in Dante. "Would you mind waiting a minute, Mr. Volkner?"

"Just don't keep me waiting too long," he said as if he were the most important man in the world.

"It won't take more than fifteen minutes. I'll be right back." Dante turned off the recorder, grabbed the folders and left in a hurry. Volkner smiled.

Dante went back to where Dr. Black and Kat were.

"I don't think he's your perpetrator," said Dr. Black.

"I agree. But there has been a string of murders over the last five years both here and in New Jersey. They were all brunettes under the age of eighteen. I need to go." Kat watched as Dante walked over to another Detective and said something to him. The detective went through a stack of folders on his desk and pulled out a thick one. They talked some more and then Dante came back to Kat and Dr. Black. He looked through the folder for a few minutes then handed it to Dr. Black who opened it and studied its contents.

"It fits his profile. He's also someone seeking attention so give it to him," he smiled at Dante but Kat found something about it a little creepy.

"Thanks, Dr. Black. I better get back in there." Kat hadn't said a word but was busy taking notes. But she couldn't help but admire the way how Dante did his job. Dante moved his badge to his jacket pocket then went back in with both folders and had a seat. He turned on the recorder before he started asking questions.

"Mr. Volkner, you helped me a lot. There has been a string of murders in New York and New Jersey. Whoever this man is, he had outsmarted us at every turn. He's also quite an artist because he puts make-up on the girls, and then dresses the girls in flattering outfits and then poses them. I want to show you the pictures of them and see if you recognize these girls. Is that alright?"

"Am I being held here, Dante?"

"No. You can leave anytime you want." He smiled at Volkner reassuringly. This caused Volkner to relax.

"I'd be happy to help."

"He's doing a good job, Kat," Dr. Black said in his charismatic manner.

"He usually does," she replied, while still trying to figure out what bothered her about Dr. Black.

Dante showed Volkner a picture, "Lovely, isn't she? Her

name is Mia, she was 17 in this picture. Does she look familiar? Anything you can tell us would be a big help."

"Did she use to frequent a club called Sassy's?"

"Yes, I believe she did."

"Her last name is Allegria," Volkner stated it as a matter of fact and was obviously pleased with himself.

"So, you know her?"

"You could say that," he answered smugly.

"What about this girl?"

"Her name is Maggie Albright. Isn't she beautiful?" he asked with pride.

"She is very beautiful. This man is truly an artist."

Volkner was obviously pleased by the compliment.

As Dante showed him photos of each girl, Volkner self-confidently told him information seemingly uncaring of the consequences of his actions.

When Dante was finished showing Volkner the pictures he casually said, "You've been quite helpful and I thank you for your help. This man is such an artist it will be a pleasure to find him. Do you have any idea who he might be?"

"Of course. I'm very proud of my work. I did it." Volkner was practically glowing.

"Thank you, Mr. Volkner. Is there any way I can get it in writing? After all, you don't want someone to take credit for your genius."

"I'd be delighted," he said smiling.

Dante gave him a tablet and a pen. Volkner happily started writing and it took quite a while. When he was done, he handed it to Dante. He read it and then smiled. "Mr. Volkner you're under arrest for the murder of..." Dante said, and read each girl's name. Then he read him his rights. Volkner just smiled proudly. When he was finished, he picked everything up and then made a phone call.

"We got him thanks to you, Dr. Black."

"I'm just happy to help," Black said smoothly.

"What can you give me Dante?" asked Kat.

"You can write the Canvas Killer, Peter Volkner, 31, has been arrested for the deaths of seven girls. You have their names."

CHAPTER FOURTEEN

HOW DARE YOU?

By Katherine Hope The New York Light

The serial killer known as the Canvas Killer apprehended

November 16th

The rapes and murders started five years ago and baffled police from both New Jersey and New York State. Peter Volkner 31, a.k.a. The Canvas Killer was caught this morning and gave a full written confession, including details not released by the police. His victims are: Mia Allegria, 16, of Brookhaven, New York; Elizabeth Albright, 17, of Rochester, New York; Sophia Ekner, 15, of Spring Lake, New Jersey; Avery Kade 17, of Cambridge, New York; Emma Leighton, 16, of Delmar, New York; Zoey Penton, 14, of Ocean Grove, New Jersey; and Willow River, 15, of Greenport, New York. Volkner earned his nickname because he posed each girl after applying make-up and dressing them in flattering outfits. Dr. Byron Black, Psychiatrist, was instrumental in catching Volkner by providing Det. Dante Russo of the 13th Precinct with interrogation techniques. Dr. Black has volunteered to help us catch the man known as The Chemist. I warned him that he would have to be careful because The Chemist is watching everyone involved in the case.

~***~

Dante called.

"How would you like to go out to dinner to celebrate?" asked Dante.

"I'd love to."

"Would seven be fine?"

"I'll be ready." And she realized she would be. Since she had received that phone call from The Chemist on October 1st she actually felt hopeful for the first time. With Dr. Black's help, they just might catch the bastard. Then she suddenly remembered she needed a new dress. Kat laughed as she thought about how quickly her mind had jumped from serial killer to needing a new dress. But she recognized it was because of another emotion she hadn't felt in an even longer time—excitement at going on a date. After she was done shopping she caught a cab to take her back to her apartment. She realized she was humming. *Since when did you start humming*? Feeling embarrassed, she glanced at the cab driver who only seemed focused on the traffic.

Dante was there on time. He was standing by the passenger door and had opened it for her. After she was in, he closed it and then went to the driver's side and got in. "You look lovely tonight. That's the first time I've seen you with your hair down. I really like it."

"Thanks, Dante," Kat said blushing. "You look very handsome. It's nice to see you in something besides a suit." He was wearing slacks and a polo shirt.

"Thanks, Kat, you're in for a treat."

"Where are we going?"

"You'll see when we get there."

"So, it's going to be that way," Kat said smiling.

Dante gave her a mischievous grin.

"It's nice to see you smile for a change."

"I haven't had anything to smile about in a while."

"Not even meeting me?"

"If you remember we got off to a rocky start. But then you grew on me."

Kat laughed. "The same here."

Kat hadn't been on a date in a long time but instead of apprehension, she felt relaxed. It felt nice to be able to trust someone and she felt that way with Dante.

They drove to the restaurant area in the nicer part of New York. When they arrived, there was valet parking and they were at Le Voleur. Famous for its French cuisine.

"Oh, I love this restaurant. I've only been here once but the food was delightful."

"I'm glad you like it," Dante said obviously pleased.

They were able to get a nice table for two located in the best part of the restaurant.

"How did you manage it?"

"I helped them with a robbery so I always get the best treatment."

"Is there anybody you don't know?" Kat asked then laughed.

Dinner went well and they made small talk and enjoyed themselves and each other's company. For the first-time in a in five years she had fun being with a man. She felt like she had known him forever. Since they clicked so well Kat didn't even hesitate when they went back to her apartment. She hesitated but then invited him in. For the first time, she felt apprehensive but she was determined to overcome it. When they went inside her apartment Dante kissed her gently. She kissed him back but was hesitant.

"It's okay, Kat, we can take it slow."

Kat withdrew from his arms and walked across the living room.

"It's just hard for me because..."

Dante walked towards her but slowly. He gently reached out and caressed her face.

"I know, Kat. It's okay. I'm not going to pressure you."

She tensed up. "What do you know?"

"About what happened at the restaurant. It's okay."

"You son-of-a-bitch, you checked into me!"

"I had to. You were allowed access to police interrogations."

"You should have told me. Now get out!" she yelled.

"Kat I—"

"Are you deaf? I said get out."

Dante left without a word.

CHAPTER FIFTEEN

IS THE DOCTOR IN?

The next day Dante called her all business. "I have some bad news. I was told to back off my investigation into your phone being bugged. Apparently, it came from up high."

"Damn it! I'm sure the investigation on this end is going nowhere also but I don't understand why. I'm pretty sure if I asked I wouldn't get an answer. "

"I don't understand it, either. I do have some good news. We have a new suspect. Want to be here for the interrogation?"

"I'll be there as soon as I can."

The Sargent at the front desk waived through and she headed straight for the interrogation room. When she got there Dante was waiting along with Dr. Black. "Talk to me," Kat said to Dante.

"Right now, he's just a person of interest but he fits the profile. Dr. Black picked him out. He's been very helpful. His name is Norman Adler, 33, 5'10", light brown hair and he worked at Richmond Chemicals Inc. up until two months ago."

"Two months ago, would be about the time the Chemist started," Kat said. She was trying not to get her hopes up. After what had happened to Jimmy she wasn't jumping to any conclusions. "Does he have any priors?"

"He's got a juvie record we're trying to get unsealed."

"That should be interesting."

"We'll see. I'm going in now, but I'll leave the speakers on so you can hear everything."

"Thanks, Dante." He smiled at her and then headed inside the interrogation room. It was the same one she'd been in.

"Can I get you anything, Kat?" she turned to see Steve standing there, Dante's partner.

Ever since that day on the docks she had disliked him.

"I'm good." Then she turned her attention back to the interrogation.

Dante sat in the metal chair across from Norman and didn't say anything for a minute as he reviewed the file in front of him. Kat was sure he already knew what it said.

"Hello, Mr. Adler. How are you today?" Dante said affably.

But Adler wasn't buying it. "I'd be better if I knew why I am here."

"We need your help. But first I'd like to ask you a few questions, if you don't mind."

"I mind, so get to the point."

"It says here you used to work at Richmond Chemicals but got fired. Care to talk about it?"

"It was bogus. I didn't do anything wrong."

"I can believe that. Someone with your exemplary record must make a lot of people jealous."

"That's exactly what happened. My boss was jealous. I was trying to find a better way to treat the common flu since the vaccine doesn't work 100% of the time. The flu kills a lot of people each year, especially the elderly and children." His manner seemed sincere.

"Can you prove that's what happened?"

"All my notes are still at the lab."

"We'll try to get access to them."

"Good luck with that. Richmond won't reveal that information."

"They will with a warrant."

"That won't help."

"Why do you say that?"

"The file is long gone by now."

"If they thought it was valuable why would they get rid of it?"

"I said the file was gone, not the information. They've hidden it under something else while they work on it."

"We'll try anyway to see if we can exonerate you. A man such as yourself deserves credit for his hard work."

This caused a reaction from Adler. "You'd do that for me?"

"Of course, but I was hoping you can help me. We've had a series of murders and we hope you can help us with them."

Adler became suspicious again. "Am I a suspect?"

"After observing this man, I don't believe he's our killer," said Dr. Black. "Is there any way to get Det. Russo's to come out here?"

"I'll get him," said Steve. He pushed a button for the intercom. "Detective Russo would you step outside, please."

"Detective Russo, he doesn't fit the profile after all. I don't think he's our killer," Dr. Black informed Dante.

"What do you suggest?"

"Continue questioning him and see if he is guilty of any crimes."

"No offense, Dr. Black, but I'm not ready to rule him out. I'm going to continue with my interrogation." Dante went back into the interrogation room and sat down.

"Can you provide alibis for the morning of October 1st?"

"Are you kidding? Who can remember that far back?"

"What about October 14th and 16th?"

"The best I can do is look at my credit card charges."

"How soon can you provide that information?"

"I can do it right now if you'll let me use my phone."

"I was in Newark on the 1st, and on the 14th through 16th I was staying in New Rochelle."

"Can you provide written records?"

"Am I a suspect for a crime?"

"Do you know Susan Blake and Mary Monroe?"

"Never heard of them."

"You sure about that?"

"I'm positive."

"Let's see how your alibis check out. Do you give us permission to check your credit card and bank statements?"

"Yes."

"Let's get that in writing."

Dante left the room. "Steve, can you get a consent form?"

"Sure."

"Kat do you recognize his voice?"

"No, but isn't it possible he's disguising it somehow?"

"Yes, that's definitely possible."

Just then Steve returned with the waiver form. "Thanks, Steve."

Dante went back into the room with Norman.

"Here it is. Sign at the bottom and put the date."

Norman signed the waiver. "Can I go home now?"

"Yes. But don't go anywhere."

"Where am I going to go?"

Norman left and so did Dante.

"You let him go?"

"We don't have enough to charge him with until we get his credit card statement and that won't be until tomorrow."

"What if he runs?"

"If this guy is The Chemist he'll have covered his tracks and thinks he's too clever to get caught. He'll slip up somewhere."

"I'm glad you're so confident."

"It's my job, remember."

"I'll call you as soon as I know something. Just go back to work and try to relax."

Kat laughed. "You've never worked at a newspaper before."

"No, but I'm a cop."

"Thanks. Dante."

Neither one said what they were thinking. It was time for The Chemist to kill again.

Kat went back to work.

CHAPTER SIXTEEN

SECRETS?

Kat finally got a break on the slum lord, Mike, "The King," Wilson.

One of the people that worked for the city council had called and left a tip that Councilman Jones was accepting bribes to look the other way and that he had paid of Detective Stoke off. But Kat couldn't concentrate. She kept waiting for his call.

The phone rang.

"Hi, Kat just wanted to keep you updated. Adler's alibis don't check out. But we still don't have enough to arrest him. His juvenile record didn't prove helpful. It seems he had some minor possession charges but that was it. We're going to bring him back in for further questioning. You want me to call you when we've picked him up?"

Kat hesitated. *What about the call from The Chemist? To hell with him, I'm not going to let him control my life. That's what he wants.* "Yes, call me."

She went back to her story and started writing. Kat was almost done when the phone rang. Thinking it was Dante she answered. "Hi, Dante."

But it wasn't him.

"Hello, dear." The Chemist's voice sent chills up her spine or something like that.

"What do you want."

"I think you know."

"Why can't you find someone else to call. I have bigger stories to write about."

"You shouldn't say things like that. What's Jimmy's wife's name? Marge, isn't it?"

"I'm sorry. I didn't mean it. What do you have to tell me?"

"The next body is at an apartment building in one of The Boss' buildings; Building two, Apartment 4-32B. You know the rules. Come alone." He hung up.

She called Dante and told him what was going on.

"I'm going with you."

"You can't. He'll know."

"Then I won't be far behind."

"What about Adler?"

"They're searching his house looking for clues now."

"I better get going."

"Just be careful."

"I will."

Kat took a ride to the apartment buildings and was once again horrified by what she saw. But unlike Cassandra Bay, she only had some people staring at her. She thought of her article about the slum lord Mike Wilson and decided to make it a priority. Kat had no problem locating the apartment. After no one responded to her knocks, Kat checked the door and it was unlocked. The girl was the first she saw and she was tied to a chair like the others. For some reason, she looked even more horrendous than the rest because she was so young. Dante answered on the first ring and was there in a matter of minutes.

"What a shame. I put in a call to the Crime Scene Unit. As soon as they're here I'm taking you back to the paper."

"No, I've still got a story to write and I need to be here."

"I can call you with the details."

Kat hesitated. "You sure you'll tell me everything?"

"I promise."

"I want to go with you to the morgue."

It was Dante's turn to hesitate.

"Alright."

"Kat took pictures of the girl and the apartment. When the CSU Team arrived, she watched as they performed their job and took pictures.

"Come on Kat. It's time to go."

Without a word, she followed him out to his car and he drove her back to the newspaper. She felt numb. Then the phone rang.

"I thought I told you to come alone."

How could he know? "I was alone."

"Don't lie to me or there will be consequences."

"I was afraid after what happened at Cassandra Bay."

"I won't let anything happen to you. I'm not ready yet."

"What does that mean?"

"I think you know, dear."

Then he hung up.

Something was bothering her more than usual. She called Dante.

"I think he slipped up."

"How?"

"I'm not sure yet but it'll come to me."

"Can I come over tonight?"

"It depends on how late I'm done. What do you know yet?"

"She fits the profiles of the other two girls. Five-sevesn, 125 pounds, hair midway down her back, green eyes."

"Do you know her identification yet?"

"We got a hit on her fingerprints. She's Adrian Jones daughter of Councilman Martin Jones."

"What did you say?" Kat asked stunned.

"Which part?"

"The Councilman."

"Councilman Jones."

"Oh, God, how could he know?"

"Know what? You're not making at sense."

"I'm writing a story about the Councilman taking bribes."

"We're going to have to do a sweep of your office and look for bugs and cameras. Besides him, who have you told?"

"Only my editor. You don't think that he's connected somehow?"

"Right now, I'm not ruling anyone out. Do you still need to take a trip to the morgue?"

"Yes. I do. I need to look at her again."

"Kat—"

"No Dante. I need to go. It's important."

"I'll pick you up in fifteen minutes."

Fifteen minutes went by and then thirty and no sign of Dante. Kat called Steve.

"Dante was supposed to pick me up fifteen minutes ago to take me to the morgue. I haven't heard from him and he's never done that before."

"I'm not sure how long ago he left but he told me he was on his way to get you. All our cars have a GPS tracker on them so I'll call you as soon as I can find something out."

She waited anxiously, and when the phone finally rang, her hand darted for the receiver. "Steve?"

"Hello dear."

CHAPTER SEVENTEEN

THE GOOD SAMARITAN

"Did you do something to him," Kat asked, trying not to show her fear.

"Not yet. But I have to make him pay."

"Pay for what?"

"For stealing your heart."

"I don't know what you're talking about. We're just friends."

The Chemist laughed and then hung up.

Kat called Steve. "We tracked his car but there was no one in it."

"Oh, God, he's going to kill him."

"Who is, Kat?"

"The Chemist, he's trying to punish me."

"But for what and what does it have to do with Dante?" asked Steve.

Kat hesitated, she didn't want to tell, especially with the way it had ended.

"We went on a date."

"Oh, I see. I'll alert everyone that we're looking for The Chemist but we don't have much of a description to go on."

Then it finally clicked. "He's the Good Samaritan!"

"Who?"

"Pull up the record on the fire at Chung's Restaurant in Chinatown. The restaurant was set fire to and a family of five were killed. It was five years ago on June 23rd."

"I still don't get it. Where does The Good Samaritan come in?"

Kat didn't want to say it. She hadn't spoken about that day for a long time. But Dante's life was at stake. "Because I was in that building too and he rescued me. Then he came to see me at St. Joseph's. I was pretty out of it but it was the way he called me dear."

"Okay, thanks, Kat. We'll get on it right away."

"Keep me posted please."

"I will."

Kat waited anxiously for Steve to call but it was night time and she hadn't heard from him so she called him.

"Sorry, Kat. I don't have any news. We looked into the Good Samaritan but he gave a fake name at the crime scene. I assure you we're doing everything we can. We've got half the police force looking for him."

Kat didn't want to say out loud what she was thinking. *What if it was too late?*

She tried to focus on her story about his latest victim, Adrian Jones but it was of no use.

Steve called her around 7 p.m. "No news. I'm sorry. I'm going to send a squad car to take you home."

"Thanks, Steve. It's kind of pointless though, since I know I won't be able to sleep."

"I know how you feel, but the way I see it, we have to be on our game tomorrow for when we hear from Dante. Don't give up, Kat. I've never known anyone tougher than Dante."

"Thanks, Steve."

It wasn't long before a police car showed up and took her home. After the officer's swept her apartment she said good night to them and they left. Kat had seen the note but didn't say anything. As soon as they were gone she went to get the note and she was in such a hurry she nearly knocked the vase over. It read: come to the city morgue alone if you want to find lover boy.

"Oh my God. Please no." She tried to call Murphy but he didn't respond. In a near panic, she phoned a cab company and told the dispatcher that it was an emergency. When the cab arrived, she climbed in as fast as she could, "224 West 35th Street. I'll pay double if you can get there in under 20 minutes."

"You got it."

When they arrived 18 minutes later, Kat paid him, exited the taxi and ran for the entrance. "Please don't let it be locked," she said under her breath. It wasn't. She opened the door and sprinted down the stairs but it seemed like she was running in slow motion. When she reached the hallway, she didn't slow down. Kat didn't even notice the smell of the formaldehyde.

As soon as she entered the room the first thing she saw was the body on one of the cold, stainless steel tables. She let out a deep sob. "No!". Time seemed to slow down as she walked towards it. Kat didn't realize how badly she was shaking. As she reached the table her vision was so cloudy from the tears streaming down her face, it took a minute for her to realize it wasn't Dante. It was Murph. Even though she was sure he was dead she checked for a pulse anyway. There wasn't one. "I'm sorry Murph," she said to his corpse. "Where's Dante?" she asked as if he could somehow tell her.

Then, she saw something white sticking out between Murph's lips. Hesitantly she reached for it and gingerly removed it from between his teeth. Kat unfolded the paper and read: check the drawers. Still sobbing, she turned and looked. There had to be at least 30 drawers. She went to the first, opened it and slid the body out. It was an elderly woman. She went to the next, then the next, methodically opening each drawer and looking. Each one holding a cold lifeless shell of someone's beloved. She didn't know how many she opened until she opened a drawer, slid the body out and started to move it back when something stopped her. Kat stared at the man's face. His skin was deathly white, his lips blue and she could barely recognize him but it was Dante. A deep sob erupted from her body as she reached for his motionless hand. "Dante, I finally found you and now you're gone."

As the sobs tore through her essence the strangest thing happened. She was crying so hard she almost didn't notice it. His hand moved. Even though she knew that corpses could spontaneously move for some time after death, she wanted to believe it meant he was alive. "Please," she begged, as she checked for a pulse. She couldn't feel anything and started to give up when she realized there was one. It was just very faint. "Thank you, God," she whispered and then pulled out her phone and pressed 911. "I need an ambulance at the city morgue. He's alive."

CHAPTER EIGHTEEN

BACK FROM THE DEAD

Kat took out blankets and layered them on top of Dante and then laid her upper body across his, further attempting to warm him up. She didn't know how long she was in that position, speaking soothing words to him, when she felt a man's hand on her arm. "Please move out of the way, Miss."

"He's alive. Check his pulse."

The paramedic looked at her like she was insane but decided to humor her. He checked Dante's body for a pulse. "Oh, my God. He really is alive!" the Paramedic exclaimed.

"Let's get him on the gurney and start warming him back up," he said to his partner. But he just stood there.

"Randy, get the gurney over here. Now."

"Sure thing, Wade," he said as if he were waking from a dream.

"What hospital are you taking him to?"

"Rose General," responded Randy.

Kat watched as they removed Dante from the drawer and put him on the gurney.

"I'll get him, Wade. Check the body on the table."

"He's gone," Kat told him.

"Yes ma'am, but we have to check anyway."

"He's dead," she heard Wade say.

"Let's go." They pushed the gurney down the hallway, took the elevator up one flight and then got him into the back of the ambulance.

"For fuck's sake! There really was a live guy in the morgue."

"Shut up and let's go," Randy told the female paramedic that was driving.

Kat got in with them. "Ma'am, we're not allowed to let you ride with us."

"But—"

"Shut the hell up, Wade. I think we can make an exception."

Kat watched them start an IV and then put a heated blanket on him, while they continued examining him.

"Crap!" Kat said as she started to look for her cell phone before realizing it had been in her hand the whole time. She tapped the keys on her phone and listened to it ring on the other end. Then someone answered.

"Steve, he's alive."

"Where are you?

"On the way to Rose General."

"I'm on my way."

When the ambulance arrived and took Dante into the ER, Kat heard someone say, "Is that the dead guy that came back to life?"

"Shut up stupid. He wasn't dead to start with. Damn morgues screw up all the time. I wonder how many people get buried alive?"

"Fuck that. It's a good thing I work here cause all the docs know I'm too damn stubborn to die."

"Are you related to him?" a nurse with a nametag that read Stacy asked Kat.

"I'm his girlfriend." The words seemed strange to her as soon as she said them.

"What's his name?"

"Dante Russo, he's a Detective at the 13th Precinct."

"Next of kin?"

"I have no idea but I'm sure when Steve gets here he can tell you."

"Who's Steve?"

"I am, nurse." Kat turned around and saw him standing there, looking at Dante's unmoving body.

"You sure he's okay?" he asked in disbelief.

"We're still checking him out. We need to run some tests in order to determine what's going on. Can you fill out this form so we can contact his next of kin?" Stacy asked as she handed him a clipboard holding a stack of forms.

"I've already called his parents. I'm sure they can fill them out as soon as they get here."

"Yes, sir. Let them know to go to Exam Room Three as soon as they arrive."

"Yes, nurse."

Kat had watched Dante disappear into a room accompanied by a man she assumed was a doctor and several nurses.

"Tell me what the hell happened, Kat."

Kat explained the bizarre story as more police officers started arriving, all filled with questions. Then they all parted ways as his family arrived. Steve waived them over.

"Mr. and Mrs. Russo, this is Katherine Hope, she's the one that found Dante."

"Call me Maria," Mrs. Russo said as she gave Kat a hug and a kiss on the check. "God bless you."

"Where is he?" Mr. Russo asked.

Steve pointed at the closed door, "They're still examining him and the nurse has a stack of forms for you to fill out."

"They can wait. I'm going to check on my son. Come on, Maria."

Even though they were both strong, assertive men, Kat thought Dante and his father couldn't be more different. She watched as the Doctor came out from behind the closed curtain and talked to them but she couldn't hear what he was saying. There was nothing she wanted more than to be there next to him, holding his hand. More police officers arrived and she heard the story of how she found Dante being told and retold until it bore little resemblance to the truth. Then, one of the nurses came out from the examination room and said something and the doctor and his parents went into the room in a hurry. A few minutes later a nurse came out and walked toward the waiting crowd who had suddenly become quiet.

"Is there anyone here who goes by the name Kat?"

"That's me," Kat responded in surprised.

"Could you come with me?"

"Of course," she said as she followed the nurse towards the examination room.

"He's asking for you," the nurse told her as they entered and the only thing she saw was Dante's face as he gave her a weak smile. He said something but she couldn't hear so she got close to him and leaned over. "What did you say, darling?"

"I love you."

Kat felt overcome by a sensation she didn't understand, then she felt awe and joy and fear at the same. She had seldom heard those words in her young life and coming from Dante they left her feeling humbled. Then she realized what the sensation was and her eyes grew moist as she let it wash over her. Kat leaned over some more and put her soft lips next to Dante's ear.

"And I love you," she whispered.

"We need the room," one of the nurses said. "You can sit in the waiting area here until we get him admitted."

Kat left but not without taking one more look.

"I think I need to have a talk with this young lady. It looks like Dante hasn't been telling us everything," said Maria as she gave Kat a welcoming smile.

"Can you tell me what the doctor said?" asked Kat.

"Dr. Morrow believes that Dante was given a beta blocker to slow his heart rate down and then put him in that awful place be-cause it was so cold. If you hadn't found him when you did he would have died," Maria said then paused in order to regain her composure. "They gave him something to increase his heartbeat, then warmed his body until they got his temperature up to where it should be. The doctor just wants to keep him overnight for observation but said he should be fine."

"Oh, thank you. I need to go tell all the police officers that are waiting for news."

"Come find us after that. I think we need to talk."

"I will," Kat promised even though she wasn't looking for-ward to it.

CHAPTER NINETEEN
LIGHT OUT

Kat was back at the Light trying to figure out her next move when she got a call from Dante that morning.

"Aren't you supposed to be resting?" asked Kat.

"I feel great, why should I rest? Besides, I've been put in charge of a task force to catch the bastard."

"You will."

"You want to have dinner tonight?"

"I'm sorry, Dante. I've got so much work to do here." There was a long pause on the other end of the line.

"Are you avoiding me, Kat?"

"No, of course not," she lied. He hadn't brought up what he said to her in the hospital and neither did she.

"I know my parents can be pushing and overbearing but they really want to get to know you better. Plus, they want to thank you again for saving my life."

Kat remained silent for a moment then she said softly, "Everybody keeps thanking me, but everyone seems to forget that you wouldn't have wound up there if it weren't for me. After Jimmy, I should have known better."

"So, you are avoiding me. How many times do I have to tell

you it's not your fault? He's a psychopath that is fixated on you for some reason. I was just convenient."

"Well don't do that again, okay?"

"Do what?"

"Be convenient."

"Well, Kat if I could figure out how he got to me in the first place, I would know how to prevent it from happening again."

"Still no clue?"

"None, and we've been going over everything. They even tried hypnosis on me but I still don't remember anything past getting in my car. I'd sure as hell like to know what kind of drugs this guy is using."

"You and everyone else."

"I better go. I have work to do."

"Wait!"

"What's wrong?"

"I just wanted to know if I could do a story about the task force. I think the public needs to know."

"I agree. I'll call you later."

Kat started writing her article on Councilman Jones. She had talked to Brad who felt that the story was too important not to run now, even though the Councilman had undergone such a tragedy.

The phone rang. "I'm proud of you."

"Even though you didn't win?"

"I have to admit you surprised me."

"What do you want?"

"Just to let you know I have a surprise for you." He hung up.

Kat called Dante and told him what the Chemist said.

"You're getting round-the-clock protection."

"I think he will find a way to get to me regardless of what you do."

"Don't think like that."

"I told you before, I'm a realist."

"You stay at the paper until officers show up. I'm having two officers assigned to you at all times."

"Dante you need to rest."

"You're more important."

Kat waited until the officers came to take her home in a squad car. When they reached her apartment, she waited outside while they went in to clear it. That was the last thing she remembered.

CHAPTER TWENTY

NIGHTMARES

Kat was feeling groggy and had a difficult time focusing. There was something hard beneath her. As she tried to look around everything seemed surreal. Then, she felt a wave of nausea and thought she might vomit but somehow managed not to. Her vision was very blurry but she was able to make out metal bars beneath her. Struggling, she managed to sit up and look around. She was locked in a steel cage. Instead of feeling frightened she started laughing. The euphoric feeling made her feel detached and she hoped it would last forever. Then she heard him but instead of her usual sense of dread, she didn't care.

"Don't worry, Kat. I'm not going to hurt you. I have quite a treat for you." The Chemist laughed but she didn't feel frightened even though a part of her knew she should. Kat tried to focus but couldn't find him. She started laughing.

"I can't see you," she said in a sing-song voice.

"I'm right here," he said then leaned forward from the shadows. But all she could make out was a black head with moving lips.

"You look weird. What's wrong with your face?" she asked, then giggled. "Have you got a secret?" She gasped as a thought crossed her befuddled mind. "Is it Halloween?"

"Yes, dear, it is." It was his turn to laugh. But for some reason, she wasn't amused.

"My head feels weird." Her vision was worse because all she could make out were colorful shapes. And she didn't like them.

"How's your vision, Kiernan?"

"I can't see very well, there are all these," she paused, then suddenly screamed.

"They're faces, hideous faces and they're talking all at once. Make them stop!"

"They will. Just be patient."

"They're all telling me I'm going to die," she shuddered and started to cry.

"It's okay dear. You're not the one that's going to die."

"I'm not? Is someone going to die?" Her head was starting to clear but she couldn't shake the deep feeling of dread. She tried to look around again. From what she could tell she was in an empty warehouse.

"Why am I here?" she asked and even she could tell her words were slurred.

"I have something special planned for you. A show you'll never forget." He laughed, but in her state of mind, she didn't know why.

"What do you mean?"

"I have my next victim here and I'm going to let you watch her die so you'll know what I have in store for you. But, first, we have to let the ketamine get you right where I want you. How are you feeling?"

"I feel like something really bad is going to happen but I don't understand why. What's ketamine?" she asked almost incoherently.

"Don't worry about that."

"Who are you?"

"I'm The Chemist, my dear. Look around and tell me what you see."

Kat's vision made her feel like she was on a see-saw. Sometimes she could see things clearly but then her vision would become blurry again. Kat managed to make out a shape and put everything into grasping what it was. Finally, she said with a trembling voice, "I see a girl. What is she doing there?" The feeling of dread had returned and her fear started to well up until she found it unbearable.

"She's unconscious, waiting for you."

The man's voice seemed to be coming from all around her. "I need to see your face. I need to know you're real."

He laughed. "I'm very real, Kat dear. But it's in your best interest not to see my face. I'm going to turn the light on now."

She heard the sound of a flick but it resounded through her head.

As her eyes adjusted to the light she saw that the woman was tied to a chair. She looked quite young. Kat realized she wasn't moving. Is she dead?" she asked, as the fear still had hold of her and the darkest thoughts crossed her mind. She shivered.

"Not yet, dear. Now, just watch, I'm heading towards the girl."

Kat's mind was so overwhelmed she needed a release. "No!" she screamed. "What are you going to do?"

"I'm going to give her an injection of adrenaline so she'll wake up. Now listen closely to my voice and hers."

Terrified, she could do nothing more than watch, no matter how much she wanted to turn away.

The Chemist gave her the shot through the IV he had connected to her arm. Almost instantly the girl woke up and started looking around.

"Where am I? Why am I tied up?" she asked. The horror in her voice was palpable.

"Lydia dear, you're going to be the star in my show."

"You still watching, Kat?"

He looked at her but his voice seemed covered in something black. "I'm watching."

"I know you're hallucinating and I'm going to make sure you have bad ones. But pay attention and I'll tell you what's real. I want you to experience this as if it were happening to you."

"But why?" Kat yelled. "What did I do to you? What did she do to you?"

"You dear, have proven to be a worthy opponent. She's got to die because I want you to have nightmares for the rest of your life."

"Oh, God no!" Kat bawled.

"Please don't kill me. I still don't understand. What are you going to do to me?" Lydia asked, and the realization that she was about to go through something awful must have hit her because she became hysterical.

"Shush now, Lydia. I'm just going to give you a little shot," he said as he showed Lydia the syringe. "You still watching, Kat?" He looked at her. "I'm going to give her a shot now so pay close attention."

There was no need to ask. Kat couldn't take her eyes off the girl.

Lydia started screaming when she saw the syringe, "No, please don't! No! Please, mister, I'll do anything you want!" she begged.

"Can you feel her fear, Kat? Can you hear her beg for mercy?" Then he said something that sent a chill up her spine. "I don't believe in mercy. It's a sign of weakness and I'm not weak. But then again never are you, dear." He cackled, showing his immense glee.

"I'm still watching," Kat responded, although she wished she could look away.

"I'm going to inject her with my own special formula now.

Watch closely because she's going to start screaming and jerking back and forth," The Chemist said as he injected the solution into her IV. Lydia immediately started convulsing and shrieking in agony. To Kat she looked like a monster, and her body was moving in ways that a human body wasn't meant to. She felt mortified and the sounds of the girl dying seemed to go on forever. After what seemed like an eternity the body stopped moving and the room was once again quiet.

"Did you enjoy my little treat?"

"Who was she?" Kat asked, her voice wavering.

"You'll see," he said with pleasure in his voice. "Don't worry, if you manage to get out of the cage I left a cell phone for you so you can call your detective and I won't be your only Good Samaritan. Bye now, Kat," he said as he walked towards a wooden door, then opened it and disappeared out into the sunshine. She thought she could hear the sound of a lock snapping in place, leaving her all alone with poor dead Lydia.

Kat felt dizzy and thought she would pass out but she was in shock. As reality sunk in, Kat tried to gather her wits. She knew how to pick locks due to her misspent youth. But how could he know that? She felt around outside the cage as far as her arms could reach and found a paperclip in front of the door. *Why would he make it so easy?* There was no way that was an accident or something he accidentally left behind. She picked up the paperclip, straightened out one end and then went to work on the lock. It was difficult to do since she had to manage by feel. Kat tried not to look at the body in front of her. After a frustrating hour, she managed to free herself. Ready to escape from within the iron prison she went through the doors on her hands and knees and then stood up when she was out. She went to the door and found the cell phone and called Dante.

"Kat, where are you?"

"I don't know. Some kind of abandoned warehouse. He killed a woman and made me watch. It was horrible."

"Just stay on the line and we can trace it and I can come get you."

"Okay."

The phone beeped. Kat looked at the battery; she didn't have much time.

"Dante my phone is going dead."

"We don't need much more time. Just stay on the line and keep talking to me.

"I didn't get a look at his face. He was wearing a mask. But Dante, he's the Good Samaritan." The phone beeped again.

"Dante hurry, my phone is—" There was silence on the other end. "Oh, God, I hope they can locate me," she said out loud. Then she saw it. A rat scurrying across the floor towards the body. She got up and ran and managed to shoo it away. But then she saw another and another. Kat tried to shoo them away but they wouldn't stop so she started to kick at them. She felt a terrible pain and looked to see one had bitten the top of her foot and wasn't letting go. Without hesitation, she reached down and pulled it off. It hurt like hell. She realized there was nothing she could do so, trying not to look, she back away from the body. Kat could hear their squeals as they chewed on the flesh of the poor girl. There were too many rats here for an abandoned warehouse and they acted like they were starving. She wondered if The Chemist was behind it. *He has to be*, she thought. The only way she could drown out the sounds was to put her hands over her ears. She prayed they wouldn't come after her next, since she had heard stories of rats eating people alive.

Kat sat down next to the door and focused on the thought that Dante could track her. After a few minutes she decided she couldn't just wait, she had to be proactive. Since the lighting was poor except over the body she used her hands and felt her way along the ribbed steel interior of the building. From what she could tell, it was large but she had no way of knowing just how big it was. Not that it would matter now. She kept going and then found two large overhead doors but they wouldn't budge. *And why would they*? Kat thought bitterly. Unable to bear the sight of the poor girl, she turned back the way she had come until she reached the door and sat down again.

It took all she had to drown out the sound of the rats' squeals and she was afraid if she looked she would lose it. Although she was tired, she didn't want to go to sleep just in case she heard someone outside. The hours passed and it started getting darker and cool which meant it must be night time. Eventually, she fell asleep. When she woke up it was to the sound of some of the rats. If she hadn't known better it would have sounded like they were screaming. She forced herself to look and saw at least a dozen of them on the floor, writhing around in pain. They must have reached some of her veins and ingested the poison. There weren't as many around and she had the horrible thought that they must be full—for now.

Her legs had started cramping so Kat decided to walk around the building again but this time she decided to head the other direction, towards the cage. It was lighter inside again, although still pretty chilly. At least it was daytime. She made her way towards the cage and then she reached it. With the light overhead the girl making the area brighter, she could vaguely see the shape of a window. Trying not to get her hopes up she managed with great difficulty to climb on top of the cage but the bars made it painful to crawl on so she sat down and scooted across. When she reached the area, it was just as she feared—it was locked. Then she heard a pounding on the door.

CHAPTER TWENTY-ONE

IS THERE ANYBODY OUT THERE?

"Katherine Hope, are you in there?" She heard a man's voice call out to her.

"I'm here! Wait a minute!" she yelled back as she quickly scrambled down from the top of the cage, ignoring the pain as her legs scraped across the top of the bars.

"Katherine Hope? If you're in there, please respond."

"I'm in here," she yelled as she ran across the floor. When she reached the door, she pounded on it as hard as she could. Then she yelled, "I'm Katherine Hope. Can you hear me?"

"Yes, we can. We'll have you free in a moment."

Then Kat heard a snapping sound and a minute later the door opened. After being in the darkness for so long she was blinded by the sunlight streaming in through the narrow opening.

"I'm Sgt. Jefferson. You're safe now," he reassured her. "Detective Russo wanted us to let you know he is on his way over. Are you cold?"

"Yes, I am but I'll be fine."

"And we won't be if Detective Russo finds out." He turned towards an officer standing next to him. "Brown, go get a blanket from the squad car."

Just then she heard a police officer from inside the building. "Holy crap! Sarge, you better come in and take a look at this."

The officer returned with the blanket and helped her wrap it around her shoulders.

"I'll be back as soon as I can. Officer Brown will stay with you so just let him know if you need anything, okay?"

"Thanks," she said as she waited with great anticipation for Dante. Kat could hear the men talking and then one of them came out and got in the car and she could hear him radio for CSU, an ambulance, and a bus.

What seemed like forever later she heard a siren and saw Dante and his partner pull up. Kat hurried towards him as he ran towards her and he took her protectively in his arms.

"I've got you now. You're safe with me," he said as he stroked her hair.

"Detective, I hate to interrupt but I think you need to take a look at this," said Sgt. Brown.

"Steve, go take a look, I'm staying here with Ms. Hope."

"Sure thing Dante," he said, and then followed the Sargent inside.

"Are the two police officers alright? I don't remember what happened."

"They're going to be alright physically, but after I get through with them they're going to wish they weren't."

"Dante, I'm sure it wasn't their fault. Please tell me what happened."

"They were hit with a tranquilizer dart. It knocked them out almost immediately. We can't determine what the drug was, though. Usually, they take a while to work."

"He got me with something, too."

"After the paramedics check you out I'm going to take you home," Dante told her.

"I need to give my statement first."

"It can wait until tomorrow."

"But Dante—"

"No, Kat. You've been through enough."

"You're right. I don't think I can deal with this right now."

"I'm here now," he said as he gave her a warm smile.

"Here's the ambulance. Let's get you checked out."

"Dante, he drugged me," Kat told, and started shaking as she remembered some of the horrors she'd seen.

He put his arm around her waist as he murmured, "I've got you. He can't hurt you."

"I know," she said as she took comfort in that.

"Do you know the name of the drug? It's important

Kat." "It started with a k or a c."

They arrived at the ambulance. "She needs to be checked out thoroughly. There's a drug that starts with a C or a K that was given to her."

One of the paramedics got her inside the ambulance while the other started checking her vitals. "What's your name, ma'am?"

"Katherine Hope."

"Hi, Katherine. My name is Shayne and my buddy here is Juan. Can you describe the symptoms?"

"I can't remember much except the horrible hallucinations. At least I hoped they were hallucinations," Kat said as she tried not to think of them.

"Do you remember feeling groggy and disoriented?"

Kat struggled to remember, "Yes, I think so, and then a kind of euphoria."

"Was the name of the drug ketamine?"

Kat nodded her head.

"The good news is that it has no lasting effects and you seem fine. All your vitals are normal. Do you have anything for anxiety or to help you sleep?"

"No."

"Then come with us to the hospital and we'll get a doctor to give you prescriptions for them."

"No, I just want to go home," Kat said adamantly.

"Stay here for a minute. I need to let the Sargent know we're leaving."

Kat reached out and grabbed Dante's arm to stop him. She looked frightened.

"It's okay, Katherine," Shayne told her. "You'll be fine here with us."

"I'll be back in a few minutes, Kat. I promise," Dante said reassuring her.

She released his arm. "Go ahead."

Dante gave her a gentle kiss on the cheek, then left. She reached up with her hand and touched where he had kissed her.

A few minutes later he was back. "You can give your statement tomorrow. Let's go."

CHAPTER TWENTY-TWO

IT'S ABOUT TIME!

They arrived back at Kat's apartment and she was surprised to see it was only 12:30 p.m.

"Do you want to get some rest?"

"No, I'm afraid to close my eyes."

"I'm so sorry you had to go through that."

Then Kat turned to Dante and put her head against his chest and at first tried to stifle her pain as she tried to be strong. But then raw emotion erupted as the reality of what she'd been through burst forth and her cry was like that of a tortured animal. Her whole body shook and he stood there holding her tight as her tears soaked his shirt. Then he felt her tense as she pulled away and ran to the bathroom and closed the door. She washed her face and dried her eyes, determined to not let any more weakness show.

After everything she had been through, she decided to try and free herself of the grime and went into her room and got fresh clothing, jeans, and a sweatshirt. She let the hot water run over her body and she scrubbed herself until her skin was raw. But nothing she did made her feel clean. After turning off the water she got dressed and towel dried her hair. She collected herself and then went into the living room to face Dante. She hated the idea that he must think her weak and was determined to show him that she wasn't.

"Would you like something to drink? I have red wine and bottled water but I can make coffee and tea," Kat said, trying not to look at him.

"Kat why don't we just sit on the couch and relax. I'm sure you have interesting stories you're writing about."

"I don't want to discuss work," she said emphatically. It made her think of him and she couldn't bear that thought right now.

"You want to watch some TV?"

She shook her head no. He was trying hard she could tell, but she felt lost.

"Maybe we should go back to the precinct so I can give my statement and get it over with."

"I don't think that's a good idea."

"That's my decision. Not yours."

"Are you sure?"

"I don't know. I'm not sure of anything since this monster came into my life."

Then she turned to Dante, "Can you teach me how to shoot a gun?"

"Yes, that's not a bad idea. You need to be able to protect yourself."

"When can we go?" Kat asked.

"I don't know Kat," Dante said looking concerned.

"How about tomorrow after I give my statement? I want to get it over with."

"I'll see if I can get someone to cover for me."

Then she thought of him not being there and the idea was too much.

"I want to be the one who kills him."

"Kat that's a dangerous way to think. The man has proven to be very cunning."

"Then I'll have to out-think him."

Dante reached down to his ankle and pulled out a small gun and carefully handed it to her.

"This is my backup piece. We can go to the shooting range tomorrow but for now just aim and fire. If nothing else you'll scare him off."

"Don't you understand? I want to kill the son-of-a-bitch. He's done running my life."

"Kat, come here."

She didn't want to admit it to herself but she needed the comfort of his arms. He held her like that until she relaxed. Then he gently tilted her head back and kissed her tenderly on the lips. She responded but with a ferocity that surprised them both. Then she pulled away and she realized she was afraid as memories came flooding over her.

"Kat, you're safe with me I promise." He took her by the hand and then led her to her bedroom. He kissed her passionately. At first, she hesitated and then she felt it well up inside her and she let herself go. He pulled her sweatshirt off. She couldn't wait to undo the buttons so she ripped off his shirt. Then they fell onto the bed.

~***~

"You ready to go?" Dante asked.

Kat laughed. "Don't you need a shirt?"

"Come here you," he said as he pulled her close and kissed her.

"I could get used to that." He was smiling at her but there was a look in his eyes. Kat smiled back. "I guess we better swing by your apartment first."

"No, I keep a spare shirt at the station."

Kat thought about why they were going there and got quiet.

"It's going to be okay," he said as he grabbed her hand.

"I just don't want to have to think about it. I want to forget but once I tell the story and a police report is filed, it becomes official. And real."

"I know. But I'll make sure it never happens again."

"How he got to you, he got me when I had two police officers with me. No, the only way to stop him is to kill him. We're still going to the firing range, aren't we?"

"Of course."

When they got to the station Dante went to the locker room to change his shirt while Steve came up to her. "You here to give your statement?"

"Yes, but I'm waiting for Dante."

"Let's go to his desk and you can have a seat."

"She's not giving her statement to Det. Russo. Cohen and Ramirez are taking over the case," the Captain told him.

"What's going on, Captain?" asked Dante,

"You're involved with the main witness in The Chemist case so I've given it to someone else."

"But Captain—"

"No buts. Steve, escort Ms. Hope to Cohen's desk would you," said Captain Griffin.

Kat and Dante looked at each other, "I'll be fine," Kat told him. But she was far from fine. She followed Steve and sat down at the desk of an overweight man with a no-nonsense attitude. After over two hours of answering questions, she was almost as emotionally raw as when it happened.

"Kat, are you alright?"

"Dante, take me to the firing range. Now," she said it with anger in her voice and hatred in her eyes.

CHAPTER TWENTY-THREE

WHO'S WHO?

The next morning, Kat called Dante. "I need to see you."

"Is this a pleasure call or is it about The Chemist."

"I think I know his identity."

"I'll be right over."

Kat sat on her couch, rehearsing what she would tell Dante. She was afraid that telling him about her past would be the undoing of her budding relationship with him. And that thought was unbearable. When she heard the buzzer, she didn't even ask who it was, she just unlocked the door and waited for him. Before he had a chance to knock she opened the door.

Dante gave her a kiss and then he took her hand. "You look upset. Tell me what's wrong."

"Let's sit down first," Kat said and then went back to where she had been sitting and waited for him to sit next to her. He had brought his notebook and pen with him.

After he sat, he took her hand and said, "Talk to me."

"When the Chemist had me in the warehouse he kept calling me dear. That's what the Good Samaritan called me." He started taking notes but when she said that he stopped and looked at her. The Detective in him had taken over and he was all business.

"Okay, is there more?"

"He called me something only someone from my childhood would know plus he knew about my ability to pick locks."

Dante was tense, she could tell by his body language. "What did he call you?"

"He called me by my real name."

"What's your real name?" he asked giving her an intense stare.

"Kiernan O'Reilly."

"When did you change your name and why?"

Kat sat there and thought about it trying to put the pieces together.

"I'm not certain but what I'm about to tell you seems the most plausible." She hesitated a moment, before continuing. "It was with my ninth foster family. I kept getting moved around because I kept trying to run away. The Walkers, the family I was with, were just like most of them—they were in it for the money. I hated it so I started making plans to run away to New York City. There was a boy there, he was a year older and his name was Ross Waverly. He was an oddball and none of the other kids there would have anything to do with him. I felt sorry for him so I became friends with Ross. We made plans of running away but looking back I realize that maybe he thought we would run away together as a couple. I always knew he had a crush on me."

Kat stopped and looked at Dante. She was afraid to continue.

"Is that all?" he said in a tone she couldn't read.

"I don't think it was by chance that he rescued me from that fire. I think he had been following me. And then when he came to see me in the hospital, he said something like, "it's me, dear". I was pretty drugged up at the time so I can't be positive. I think that's when he started planning to kill me but he wants me to suffer first."

"That makes sense. Go on."

“I don’t know if you noticed but all the girls he killed fit my description.” She looked at Dante again and this time she saw a look of caring on his face.

He reached out and took her hand. “I noticed, Kat. I never said because I didn’t want to frighten you.”

“Did you really think I wouldn’t notice on my own? Long blond hair, green eyes, five-seven, 120 pounds. That’s me.”

“You left out beautiful. Why do you think he fixated on you?”

She blushed. “I guess I never looked at it that way.”

Then he became all business again. “What else?”

“I think he changed his name also.” Kat didn’t know if she couldn’t say the rest.

“Why do you say that?”

“Ross Wavery ceased to exist when he turned 18. That’s when Dr. Byron Black came into existence.”

CHAPTER TWENTY-FOUR

HOW WOULD YOU LIKE TO DIE?

"What? You really believe that?" Dante said sounding incredulous.

"He called me dear the first time we met. Don't you find that suspicious? I didn't want to believe it either until I did some checking. Won't you even consider it?"

Dante sighed. "It doesn't make sense that he'd take a chance by getting so close to us."

"He likes attention."

"You have a point. I'll check into it."

Kat sighed with relief. "Thank you."

"Why didn't you trust me enough to share your secret?"

Kat sat there and thought for a minute. "I don't know. I guess I had hidden it for so long I was in denial."

"I hope you know now you don't have to keep any more secrets from me."

"I know, but—"

"What?"

"It's just something you said in the hospital. You don't remember? When you first woke up."

"I don't remember anything. Why? What did I say?"

Kat hesitated, she was afraid to say it out loud. "You said 'I love you.'"

Dante smiled at her. "Just because I don't remember saying it doesn't change the fact that it's true."

Kat didn't realize she'd been holding her breath until she had to force herself not to gasp for air. "I love you," she said, even though those words scared her. He must have sensed it.

"Don't be afraid, Kat. I'm not going to leave you. Come here." She moved closer and leaned her head on his shoulder. They sat that way for a while just enjoying each other's company. Then Dante's phone rang and he answered it.

"Yeah, Steve what's up?" Dante listened for a while. "Alright, I'll be right there."

"What is it?" Kat asked.

"We just received a tip about who The Chemist might be."

"Who's that?"

"I'm not sure. Steve just said to come right away."

"Are you going to pursue what I told you about Dr. Black?"

"Of course. I'll call you later."

But she didn't believe him. She got out her phone and called information and wrote down the number in her notebook before being transferred.

"Westwood Mental Health Group."

"I'd like to make an appointment with Dr. Black."

"Have you been seen by him before?"

"No."

"Then you need an hour-long appointment for an assessment. Would tomorrow at 9 a.m. work?"

"Yes."

"And your name?"

"Kiernan O'Reiley."

"Be here ten minutes early so you can fill out your medical forms."

"I will. Thank you."

Kat went in her bedroom, got out the gun Dante had given her and waited. An hour later he called. "I understand you want to see me? I would think by now you'd realize how dangerous that is."

"You're going to kill me anyway so what have I got to lose."

He laughed with a dreadful glee. "I'm going to thoroughly enjoy watching you die. But you don't get to pick when."

"Can I ask you some questions?"

He didn't even pause. "Where do you want to meet?"

"Why don't you come over?"

"So, you can set a trap for me?"

"I know you're too smart for that."

"You're right. There's nothing you can do to outsmart me. I'll be over in 30 minutes."

Kat put the gun in the back waistband of her jeans, put on a top long enough to hide it and waited.

Thirty minutes later he opened her door and walked in.

"Hello, Ross."

"I haven't heard that name in a long time."

"Why'd you change your name?"

For the first time since she'd known him he got angry.

"Because you left me, bitch," he said, menacingly.

Kat laughed. "You shouldn't take things so personally. You were just some dumb kid. Did you really think I'd wait for you?"

He went into a rage and raised his hand to hit her and then stopped and composed himself. "Nice try but you're only baiting me so I'll lose control." He smiled at her and she thought she liked his anger better.

"How'd you get Jimmy to leave the building unprotected?"

"I've decided I'm ready to kill you now so I'll humor you first. I called him and told him that if he didn't come I'd kill you."

When Kat heard that, the pain was palpable. Then she reminded herself she had to stay in control. "How'd you get Mary Monroe's body in the apartment in Cassandra Heights?"

"Aren't you the curious one? You know that really is an easy one. There's nothing that drug addicts won't do for money." He smiled at her again. That smile that showed his perfect white teeth, but somehow managed to look malevolent.

"How did you—"

"Shut up. I'm tired of your questions. Now I have one for you."

"What's that?"

"How would you like to die?"

"Quickly, I—"

CHAPTER TWENTY-FIVE

SURPRISE!

When Kat woke up she was tied to a chair. She knew what happened next but also knew that if she wanted to live she had to keep her composure. As she looked around she realized she was in the same building with the cage. That meant the rats. Then she realized in his overconfidence he hadn't checked her for a weapon. Of course, why would he? She just learned how to use one. And it was still in her waistband. If she could only figure out how to get out of the ropes but they were pretty snug.

"Couldn't come up with anyplace more original than this, Ross?"

"Don't call me that. My name is Byron."

"If that's what you say, Ross."

"You're about to die and all you can do is try and play mind games?" He sounded annoyed.

"I'm not afraid to die."

"Of course you are!" he screamed at her.

"No Ross, I'm not."

He picked up a syringe. "You know what this is?"

"Your secret magical potion?"

He slapped her so hard the chair tipped over and she hit her head on the cold, cement floor. For a minute she thought she'd lose consciousness but managed to hold on. He was saying something. Kat tried to focus.

"Look what you made me do." He tried to stand the chair back up but she went limp and became deadweight which proved to be too much for him. He screamed and then kicked her so hard in the stomach she almost screamed in pain. She forced herself to hold it in.

"Maybe I'll just leave you here for the rats." He laughed obviously quite pleased with himself.

"You mean those cute furry little creatures?" she managed to say.

"You fucking bitch!"

He tried pulling her upright again and she went limp. But she felt the ropes slip. This time he managed to get her upright but it left him out of breath.

"You're spoiling everything, you fucking whore."

"Come on, Ross. You can do better than that."

"Shut up!" he screamed then slapped her again as hard as he could. The chair started to tip but he grabbed at it catching it by the ropes and loosening them enough that they came off. She pulled out her gun.

"Are you afraid to die, Ross?"

She looked into his stunned eyes and pulled the trigger.

EPILOGUE

What did you find out Dante?"

"I talked to the police in Basin City. His mother was killed by his father, and it was pretty gruesome although they never did find out the cause of death."

"You think it was poison?" asked Kat.

"It could have been. His father was a chemist."

"That makes sense. So, what happened to the father?"

"They don't know, he disappeared. But this is the sad part. Ross stayed in the house with his dead mother for over a week. It wasn't until someone noticed the smell that they found him. He had an aunt but, apparently, she didn't want him so he wound up in foster care."

"That could turn someone into a monster."

"Maybe. But I think it was the culmination of everything that turned him into a killer."

"I guess we'll never know.

IF YOU LIKE THIS BOOK PLEASE LEAVE A REVIEW THANK YOU

Feel Free to sign up for my newsletter at https://www.stephaniecolbert.co I'll try to make it a good time for everyone!

Made in the USA
Middletown, DE
21 December 2018